Rebecca McConkey

TRUE STORIES of the AMERICAN FATHERS

for the GIRLS and BOYS ALL OVER the LAND

Rebecca McConkey

TRUE STORIES of the AMERICAN FATHERS
for the GIRLS and BOYS ALL OVER the LAND

ISBN/EAN: 9783741124716

Manufactured in Europe, USA, Canada, Australia, Japa

Cover: Foto ©Andreas Hilbeck / pixelio.de

Manufactured and distributed by brebook publishing software
(www.brebook.com)

Rebecca McConkey

TRUE STORIES of the AMERICAN FATHERS

TRUE STORIES

OF THE

AMERICAN FATHERS,

FOR THE

GIRLS AND BOYS ALL OVER THE LAND.

BY

Miss REBECCA M'CONKEY.

"Sayings of old: which we have heard and known, and our fathers have told us: . . . that the generation to come might know them, even the children which should be born; who should arise and declare them to their children: that they might set their hope in God."—Psa. lxxviii.

Ten Illustrations.

NEW YORK:
NELSON & PHILLIPS.
CINCINNATI: HITCHCOCK & WALDEN.

9608.

Landing of the Pilgrims.

See page 64.

PREFACE.

THE Authoress of the accompanying little
volume thinks no apology necessary for
presenting to our young people an "old story."
Being a story of the "immortals," it will bear
to be retold all down the ages. She remem-
bers how her own childish imagination was
stirred with its wonders and glories; how she
found the old Greek valors and heroisms,
the statuesque Roman virtues and patriotisms,
and the romantic exploits of the "Cœurs de
Lions" of the Crusades, all paralleled in this
story of the early heroes of our own land.
Then, too, its wonders and its glories were
wrought after a loftier inspiration, and its heroisms were tuned to a higher key. The ma-
chinery of the story disclosed also the presence
and the working of the living and the true

God, who made bare his arm in the eyes of all the people.

We think no candid student of the early annals of American History can fail to be convinced that this country was committed by the God of nations into the custody of *Protestant Dissenters*, and it remains to see how they will acquit themselves of their high commission. The Western World, discovered by Columbus under the patronage of Catholic Spain, was for a hundred years following explored, mapped, and accurately described, at immense cost, by Spanish Catholic expeditions, which utterly failed to subdue or settle it. We refer, of course, to that part of the Continent which is now the United States. The French had better success in Canada, but their hold on our territory was but a chain of military outposts, without the stamina necessary to successful colonization, and all these early fell by the fortunes of war into English Protestant hands. Neither do we except the colonization of Maryland afterward by Calvert—one of the purest,

gentlest natures that ever adorned humanity—
because the colony was speedily reinforced and
filled up with Protestant immigration, so that it
soon lost entirely its Catholic identity. The
immense immigration of both devout and in-
fidelized Catholics of the last days is rather
matter of regret than felicitation, for assimila-
tion has not kept pace with growth, and an
inevitable constitutional weakness is the result, that painfully suggests the image of the
Prophet's vision, "part iron and part clay."
Yet to-day the country is still the heritage of
Protestant Dissent.

While these views are not disguised in the
little historical sketches we offer, we trust we
have "set down naught in malice," and that no
sectional bitterness will be found to disfigure
these pages, which, written for the young, ought
to breathe only "peace and good-will."

CONTENTS.

CHAPTER IX.

CHAPTER X.

CHAPTER XI.

CHAPTER XII.

CHAPTER XIII.

CHAPTER XIV.

CHAPTER XV.

Contents.

CHAPTER XXI.

CHAPTER XXII.

Illustrations.

TRUE STORIES

OF THE

AMERICAN FATHERS.

CHAPTER I.

The Discovery—Christopher Columbus.

THE hands of the library clock were at the
stroke of six ; the children were gathered
round the table awaiting with eager faces
Aunt Edith's appearance. The chill December
winds that swept the lawn and portico put an
early stop to their out-door sports, and drove
the little folks to seek their pleasures at the fireside. The household at " Perry Hall " was a
well-regulated one, and the supper-bell rang
promptly at seven. It had been the children's
custom to spend the hour preceding this in
story-telling and story-listening, with their father. But he was to be absent this winter : he
sat in the national councils, mending and making the laws of the land. The mother was a
confirmed invalid, and could only bear a short

visit each day from her children. The sole
hope to make the library-hour a pleasant one
was in Aunt Edith, whose rare gift for story-
telling was beyond dispute. She had actually
promised, if they would consent that it should
be an hour of instruction as well as entertain-
ment, to tell them some true stories, which
every little American boy and girl ought to
know, and to try to tell them so simply that
even "Stevey" would understand them, at least
in part. They readily consented, for Albert,
fourteen, and Nannie, twelve, considered themselves too old and far too wise to listen to fairy
tales. Harry was ten, and "didn't care a but-
ton" whether the story was true or false, if it
was only a "real good story." Stevey was
eight, and would be satisfied with any story if
Aunt Edith would tell it. The clock had barely ceased striking when they heard Aunt Edith's
step on the stairs, and in another moment she
was seated among them. Stevey in his cushioned chair claimed the seat of privilege close
beside her, with his golden curls and small
white face touching her shoulder, where he so
loved to rest his weary head. Patient little
sufferer from an incurable malady, a household
angel was "little Steve"—one of those visions
let down into our homes for awhile, to be soon

received up again, drawing our hearts after them into the heavens.

Aunt Edith laid some maps upon the table, saying, " I shall talk to you this evening, dear children, about the discoverers of our country. Can any of you tell me who discovered the Western Continent?"

Harry answered, " Columbus, in 1492."

" How long ago?"

The children studied awhile, and Albert answered correctly.

" It seems a long while. Perhaps you think Columbus is dead, and we may forget him except in connection with the dry historical fact that he first discovered land in the Western Hemisphere in 1492; but I want you to let him be with us here, a fireside reality to-night, while we talk of his virtues and his splendid deeds, and the vast benefits he conferred on his fellow men without asking or receiving any reward. Harry, lift the globe and set it on the table before us. Now find Italy."

" O, aunty! he is looking for Italy in the Gulf of Mexico!" cried Nannie, laughing.

" Hold on a minute; I reckon I am coming to it," said Harry, with a sly wink; for he was an ambitious boy, and did not like to be caught napping.

"Well, get across the Atlantic as quickly as possible, and, please, don't keep us waiting," said Albert. "There, go through the Straits of Gibraltar into the Mediterranean."

"Yes, yes, here it is," cried Harry, "shaped like a boot."

"What are its boundaries, Albert!" asked Aunt Edith.

"It is a peninsula, bounded by the sea on the south, east, and west, and has Austria and Switzerland on the north.

"Naturally, then," continued Aunt Edith, "the Italians would be a sea-going, commercial people. Commerce means carrying articles from where they are grown or are made to other places where they are wanted. The Italian cities had grown rich and powerful by this carrying trade, and had the boldest, bravest sailors and navigators, though they had never gone far beyond the Mediterranean Sea, except along the northern coast of Africa, and through the Straits of Gibraltar, along the French coast, and as far north as England. Nannie, find Genoa."

"Here it is, aunty, in the north-western part of Italy, on the Gulf of Genoa."

"Very well; it is interesting to us to-night as the birthplace of Columbus. He was the son of a poor wool-comber. He had few advantages, for there were no public schools in Italy then, and indeed none at this day, where the poor man's son can grow learned without money and

COLUMBUS.

without price. His daily toil over, the thoughtful boy spent his leisure hours on the sea-shore. He loved the sea. Its murmuring waves as they rolled up to his feet brought strange tales to his young spirit of far-off lands unvisited, over the waste of waters. He sat and listened by the hour to the stories of the old sailors. Their fancies and legends were woven into his own dreams, by day and by night, until the far-off lands were almost as plain to his vision as the spires and towers of his native city, or the boats and ships in her harbor. His love for the sea overcame his fear of it, and the boy resolved that one day he would begin his ocean-journey, and sail to the setting sun in search of the lands of which he dreamed. He studied geography, and knew all the maps by heart; though, of course, they were very imperfect, and not at all like those you study from. Well, Columbus grew from thoughtful boyhood into thoughtful manhood, but he remembered "the dreams of his youth." How could he realize them? Who would believe with him? Who would furnish him ships or money, or venture out with him on the pathless, unknown waters? I cannot linger now to tell you all Columbus' difficulties and discouragements—how he was laughed at and scorned for his dreams, alike by the ignorant and the learned, in his own city and in strange cities; but none could shake his faith; it had become an inspiration. At last he made his way into the presence of the ruler of his country, seeking to kindle the royal ambition with the prospect of vast empires to be discovered and claimed in his name; but the prince's vision was dim. He had not Columbus' faith to see the unseen, and he closed his ear to his appeal. The young Italian turned away from his native land and sought favor in foreign courts. Some historians say that he appeared both at the English and French courts, but without success. Now find Spain, Harry," and Aunt Edith pointed it out to Steve on her map.

" I have it here in the south-western part of Europe."

" Very well. On the throne of Spain sat the youthful pair, Ferdinand and Isabella. Columbus gained admittance into the royal presence; he laid his maps before the king and queen, and explained his theories and gave his reasons. We have no proof that Ferdinand gave him the least encouragement, but that queenly woman, Isabella, believed with him; the fire of his enthusiasm kindled hers, and she opened her royal caskets and gave the adventurer her jewels. The jewels were sold, and the money purchased three small vessels and manned them. On the 3d of August, 1492, Columbus, with heart full of hope, sailed away from the little town of Palos, in Spain. He first went south and touched at the Canary Islands; after that he steered west. You will find those islands on the western coast of Africa, Harry."

"Yes, here they are: Canary Islands. They belong to Spain, it says on the map."

"The land now had faded away; they were alone on the wide sea—the three little vessels. They tried always to keep together, but this it was sometimes difficult to do—tempests tossed them; the deeps threatened to swallow them up. Days had grown into weeks, and weeks into months; there was nothing to be seen but sky above, and water, water every-where. Still Columbus kept his course, steering always toward the setting sun, for that was his dream. At length provisions began to be scarce; the men became weary of the monotony of the voyage, and were fearful they would never see land or home again. But Columbus had great influence over them, and persuaded them to continue their course. This happened many times, until at last they feared they would starve for want of food; and indeed there was great danger of it. They rebelled, and threatened to take Columbus' life unless he would turn back. He besought them to continue but three days longer, with the promise that if in that time no land appeared he would yield to their demands, and turn his ships' prows homeward. They had no

sympathy with the high aims and lofty purposes of the man who led them.

"Now, dear children, think of the agony of
spirit that this man must have endured for these
three days. To fail now was to fail always. If
he returned unsuccessful, who would assist him
in a second venture? how could he present himself before the noble woman who had sacrificed
so much, who had believed in him, whose name
was linked with his, either to be honored if he
succeeded, or scorned if he failed? Through
the live-long day his straining eye swept the
dim distance for some blessed line of lee-
shore, but there was none. And now the days
were done, and the shadows of the third night
came down gently on the little vessels, on the
far-stretching weary waters, and on the sad,
anxious heart of the man Columbus. This one
night was all that remained, for on the morrow
he must keep his promise; he must bury in
the deep sea the hopes of his life, and turn his
face homeward. Columbus did not sleep; no,
he paced the deck of the little vessel under the
bright stars of that tropical sky through all the
watches of the night. The stars faded back
into the sky; Columbus bared his head and
prayed—for he was a devout Catholic—that God
would take the helm, that he would show him

favor, and bring him to his desired haven. And
Columbus stayed his soul on God and trusted
in him, and even while he prayed the day
dawned, and a loud cry rang out on the morning air, from the man on the watch, " Land
ahead ! ho ! land ahead !"

The children clapped their hands and laughed
for joy.   Harry swung his cap, and called for
three cheers for Columbus ; and Albert proposed
three for Isabella, who was a great woman to
give up her jewels ; not many would.   Nannie
looked indignant, while little Grace, coming in
at the moment, jumped up and down, without
at all knowing the cause of the joy which had
made such a little uproar around the table.
After a few minutes, Aunt Edith called them to
order by inquiring if they were not curious to
know what land it was that Columbus had
found.

" It was an island," said Albert, " but the
name I don't remember."

" One of the group of Bahamas, off the eastern coast of Florida, which Columbus named
San Salvador.   Trace his course, Nannie, on
the globe."

" Due west, aunty, from Spain."

" A little south too."

" How many miles, Harry ?"

" Three thousand."

" They came to anchor some distance from the shore. How rejoiced they were now that they had not turned back! How beautiful the land looked! Birds of brilliant plumage and wondrous song flew about their ships, the rich perfume of tropical plants and fruits filled the air, while the natives, with their grotesque adornments of feathers and jewels, gathered on the sea-shore to behold the wonderful strangers, the pale-faces, not knowing whether they were gods or men. Columbus, arrayed in scarlet robes, richly embroidered, embarked in small boats with his officers and the priests who had accompanied him, all in full dress, and they rowed to the land. Stepping on shore, Columbus prostrated himself and kissed the ground. Kneeling, he planted a cross, the symbol of his faith ; the priests chanted a hymn of thanksgiving—the first Christian service on the soil of the new world ; then, rising to his feet, Columbus drew his sword, the symbol of earthly power, and claimed the discovered territory in the name of Isabella, queen of Spain.

" The natives were a gentle, docile race ; they looked upon their visitors as superiors, and offered them Indian hospitalities. The Spaniards distributed among them presents they had

brought, and they were good friends. Columbus visited other larger islands in the Caribbean
Sea, and named them West Indies, believing
them to be part of that group which were only
imperfectly known to Europeans as the East
Indies. He did not then know that a continent
and a wide ocean lay between the West and East
Indies. After exploring the various islands, and
lading their vessels with tropical fruits, birds,
spices, etc., they set sail for home, to carry the
glad tidings of their success.

"You can imagine how they were received
on their return, and how proudly and thank-
fully Columbus bent his knee, and offered his
homage to the youthful queen who had given
him her faith and her jewels. This question
that the centuries had been asking, whether the
world was round—whether other unexplored
continents lay on·its opposite side—was now
answered, and Columbus was the man who had
answered it. Others had thought so before
him, others had dreamed it, but he realized
their dream and his own. Many people think
dreamers and poets are a useless class of people, but this is a mistake. They have their
mission to perform for the good of the world ;
their brains conceive, and other men's hands
work out their conception. But Columbus both

dreamed and brought it to pass, so that his name is placed high up among the immortals. His history teaches us the lesson of fidelity to the highest thought within us. Columbus felt himself inspired to do this work, and he was faithful to that inspiration through evil as well as good report. Alas! that his history should also furnish us so sad an example of the ingratitude of those upon whom he had conferred benefits so vast.

" While he and his heroic companions received honor from many, yet there were not wanting those full of envy and malice who endeavored in every way to belittle him and steal from him the fame he had so fairly won. Among these was King Ferdinand himself, who was no doubt mortified that he had failed to recognize his greatness, and thus become known to after ages as the patron of so great a man. Though Columbus spent his life in the work of advancing human knowledge, braving the perils of the sea, twice shipwrecked, and passing months in desert lands, yet the malice of his enemies followed him to the end. From his fourth and last voyage he was brought home in chains, on some petty charge, by order of Ferdinand. He was now an old man; Isabella, his queenly patron, was dead; his constitution was shattered by the labors and perils of his life, and he gladly closed his eyes in death. Though his own generation was not worthy of him, yet after ages gave him reverence; and as long as our race endures his name will be linked with lofty wishes and mighty achievements.

"Now, Albert, you may make a list of heroes if you wish, beginning with Columbus, and I think I can furnish you with at least one new one each night."

The children thanked Aunt Edith for the story, and Aunt Edith thanked them because they had been such attentive listeners. Here the tea-bell rang, and away they all scampered into the dining-room.

CHAPTER II.

Exploration—Cabeza de Vacca—Ferdinand de Soto.

THE children had been waiting for ten minutes to hear the clock strike six. Aunt Edith came into the library just two minutes before the time, and found her little auditors all ready "to start on another voyage." But she begged them not to lose the thread of the story, saying: "I want you to consider what a state of mind Europe was thrown into when the fact was settled that rich islands and continents lay on the opposite side of the world, and within such easy reach ; for Columbus had left Spain in August, and in October had taken possession of the West India Islands in the name of Isabella. The rage for discovery seized all classes, and the spirit of romance and adventure possessed them. The kings of other European countries were now only too eager to share with Spain the possession of these western empires that promised to open such inexhaustible stores of wealth. They gladly patronized and assisted any brave and skillful navigator who would follow Columbus' example

and undertake discovery and exploration. I
want you to notice that Columbus in his first
voyage did not visit the mainland.   It was not
until his third voyage that he touched the
shores of South America, and explored most of
its eastern coast.   But North America was first
visited by the Cabots, father and son, immediately after Columbus' return from his first voyage.   They sailed from England with a patent
from the English king, to discover and claim
territory in the name of England.   They first
touched the shores of Labrador, and afterward
sailed into the bays and harbors of what is now
New England, and as far south as Virginia.
They made several voyages, thoroughly exploring the whole eastern coast of North America,
beginning at the dismal cliffs of Labrador, where
their ships were well-nigh crushed and borne
down by the icebergs.   They went on shore at
various points, learned all they could of the soil,
productions, and natives, and affixed the banner
of England to this vast continent.   The Cabots
were learned and courtly Venetian gentlemen,
but had long lived in England as merchants.
They collected much valuable information on
their voyages.   The younger Cabot spent his
life and much of his private fortune in these
expeditions, and was known and honored in

every court in Europe. He lived to extreme old age, and in his dying moments his wandering thoughts were still upon the ocean. The French king did not want Spain and England to possess all these new worlds, so he too sent out expeditions. They engaged extensively in the fisheries of Newfoundland, and traded with the Indians for furs. This brought them much wealth. They explored what is now Canada, and raised there the cross, bearing a shield with the lilies of France. The Jesuit priests set about converting the Indians. They named the noble gulf and river, St. Lawrence, after one of their martyrs. Champlain, a noble Frenchman, who was called the father of French settlements in Canada, gave his name to the beautiful lake which we sailed on last summer. Albert, where is it?"

"In the northern part of New York, between New York and Vermont, aunty." ·

"But the Spanish continued to push their discoveries with great perseverance, and claimed all the continent by right of first discovery, though this claim was never recognized by other nations. As early as 1530 the Spaniards and Portuguese had surveyed and explored all the coasts of the Gulf of Mexico. They crossed the Isthmus of Panama, and were first to look upon the broad Pacific. Expeditions from these countries, under Cortes and Pizarro, conquered Peru, in South America, and Mexico, in North America, and found out that these countries were full of gold and silver ore, and precious stones. They returned to Spain with their stolen treasures of gold and silver, trophies from these conquered empires, and they boldly affirmed that toward the north and east, in the interior of what they called Florida, which name included the whole of what is now the United States and Canada, there were other more flourishing and magnificent Indian empires, which could be conquered and plundered just as easily as those of Mexico and Peru had been.

"The imaginative Spaniards listened and believed the story. Their enthusiasm knew no bounds; great expeditions were planned; they were to carve up empires with their swords, plunder and divide their treasures at will, enslave the conquered natives, and send them home in chains. Moreover, they were to possess and hold the territory, plant colonies, and become the founders of States. No story, no legend concerning this favored world of wealth and beauty was too extravagant to be believed. Many old men joined these expeditions, hoping to renew their youth by bathing in the fabled fountains of immortality. 'Man proposes, but God disposes.' Listen to the story: Two expeditions left Spain. The first, under Narvaez, with a rich fleet of vessels, reached the coast of Florida in 1527. They disembarked and penetrated into the country in a north-easterly direction, wandering through marshes, swamps, and forests, until their numbers were wasted by fevers and famine. Dispirited by their failure at finding neither gold nor silver, they turned back toward the sea. They built small boats to bring them down the river more speedily, but upon arriving at the coast they were met by a West Indian hurricane, which wrecked or sunk their boats. A few escaped to the shore and there perished with hunger, except a noble Spaniard who had been second in command of the expedition, named Cabeza de Vacca, with three of his companions.

"This man's career furnishes an excellent commentary on the motto 'Never despair,' and his story ought to stir every boy's courage and confirm his resolution always to 'try again.' The brave Cabeza de Vacca, says the historian, 'as calm and self-possessed a hero as ever graced a fiction,' did not sink in despair nor waste time in uselessly bewailing his misfortunes; he studied the language and habits of

the Indians, peddled articles of his own manufacture from tribe to tribe, and won a great
name among them as a 'medicine man 'of wonderful gifts.'   Though completely at the mercy
of the Indians, yet he bore a charmed life—no
hand was lifted against him or his companions.
He made friends of the red men, and was welcomed as a superior being wherever he went.
For six years he lived among them, and at last
formed the resolution to penetrate the interior
of the country, taking a westward course.   He,
with his three companions and many Indian
warriors, who gladly followed the fortunes of
the man who had so fascinated them, journeyed
westward through the rich and fertile vales of
what we now know as Alabama and Mississippi
until they, first of men from the Old World,
came in sight of the 'Father of waters,' the king
among rivers—the Mississippi.   They crossed
and traveled on westward still, over the mighti-
est chain of mountains on the earth—the Rocky
Mountains—making their entire pilgrimage on
foot.   At the end of two years these brave
pioneers of the forest emerged from the wilderness, and came in sight of the Pacific Ocean,
at the village of San Miguel, in Sonora.   From
that place they went to Mexico, where they
were welcomed with great honors, which they

richly deserved. On their return to Spain they were received with high honors from all brave men and fair women. Cabeza de Vacca addressed a narrative of his adventures to the king, who bestowed upon him the title of the 'Columbus of the Continent.'"

"Well done!" exclaimed Harry. "I hope you will put his name down in the list of heroes, Albert, and I wish I could get that narrative. I should like to read every word of it."

Here Albert traced with his finger over the map exactly the course which he thought they followed, and the children were filled with wonder and admiration at such an achievement.

"Now, children, let me tell you of the second Spanish expedition under Ferdinand de Soto, who had been with Cortes at the conquest of Mexico. He was accompanied by six hundred men in the bloom of life, of whom many were Spanish nobility who had sold their houses, vineyards, and landed estates to equip themselves for this expedition, from which they were to return enriched a hundred-fold for all they had expended. A numerous body of priests also accompanied them with their gorgeous vestments and altar ornaments, for the natives were to be converted to the Catholic faith. Unfortunately they also carried chains and handcuffs to secure the captive Indians, and blood-hounds with which to track and hunt them. They had an army of horsemen and one of infantry. Thus they set off very magnificently 'with glittering armor and silk upon silk.' They landed upon the coast of Florida, near the bay of Apalachicola. Look it up, Harry, and show your map to the children. They journeyed northward and eastward. Dangers beset them. The natives, who had learned to fear and hate the Spaniards, sent many a poisoned arrow whirling through the air from their secure hiding-places. When caught by the Spaniards and questioned where gold and silver could be found, they purposely led them into swamps and morasses, up and down, so that they wearied themselves without making any progress. They were very cruel to the Indians, cutting off their fingers and hands for little cause, and throwing them to their hounds to be torn to pieces. They burned whole Indian settlements with all their stores, which caused great suffering to the natives and to themselves also, as they depended mainly upon the plunder of the Indian store-houses for their subsistence.

"They traveled through what is now the States of Georgia and the Carolinas, admiring the magnificent oaks, the graceful palmetto, the fragrant magnolias, the sweet gum, the pine, the cypress, with their festoons of vine, the multitude of birds of rare plumage and song, and many animals they had never seen before. But they found no gold, no gems, no great Indian cities with rich temples to plunder and destroy. The murderous arrows of the Indian and the autumnal fevers wasted them. They would gladly have been at home again, but they were ashamed to go. The proud Spanish chief, Ferdinand de Soto, he who had gained such glory in Mexico, could not brook the thought of failure. He had promised his followers more magnificent conquests than those of Cortes and Pizzaro, and was resolved to keep that promise.

" He continued his course gloomy and silent. Summer and winter had passed away. They turned their faces westward, crossed the beautiful Tennessee, went through the Cherokee settlements, where there was abundance of gold beneath their weary feet, but the Indians knew nothing of it. Westward still they toiled through the fertile vales of Alabama and Mississippi, until they reached the shores of 'the mighty river that comes down from the north.' It was a mile wide, with deep and rapid current. They were detained many weeks building rafts strong enough to bear their horses. They still hoped to find in the country beyond the great river the golden empires they were seeking. Their course was westward and northward, exploring the great river and its tributaries, and all that country which we call Arkansas and Missouri. They found neither gems nor gold. Despairingly they turned their steps southward and toward the river again. Three years of wanderings through forests and across rivers and marshes, Indian arrows, and the malaria of the country, had diminished their numbers to a handful. Instead of the rich and noble army of Spanish courtiers, dressed in magnificent silks, their horsemen and infantry in glittering armor of burnished steel, that started to enslave a continent, only two or three hundred exhausted, emaciated men, clothed in skins or mats of ivy or feathers, remained to De Soto.

" The proud Spaniard looked on the rushing current of the mighty river, and longed to go with it down to a sea of forgetfulness. He was a broken-hearted man. A wasting fever seized him. Calling his followers around him, he named his successor, bade them farewell, and died. The Spaniards wished to conceal his death

from the Indians, who held him in great awe.
To do this they wrapped his body in a mantle,
at midnight they rowed to the middle of the
river, and while the priests chanted a requiem
of sorrow, they silently sunk it beneath the
waters. Thus died the explorer of the great
Mississippi Valley and River, who, says the
historian, had crossed a large part of the continent in search of gold, and found nothing so
remarkable as his burial-place.

"All that the wretched remnant of De Soto's
followers could now do was to follow the river
down to the gulf. They were too weary to
march, and were five hundred miles from its
mouth. They must needs build boats—no easy
matter. They erected a forge, gathered all the
iron in the camp, struck off the handcuffs and
chains from their Indian captives, and bade
them go, melted their stirrups and spurs, and
turned all this metal into nails, and made rough
boats of logs split up. They stole from the Indians all the provisions they could find, loaded
their boats, and floated down the stream. Many
days brought them to the gulf, many more they
beat about the coasts, until few remained to be
rescued and tell the tale of their disastrous failure. It was indeed a failure from their selfish
point of view, for they were nothing more than

a magnificent band of robbers, who proposed only to enrich themselves, But it was not really a failure, for they had explored the interior of a vast continent, and preserved and carried back to Europe correct maps and accounts of it. Human knowledge was advanced, and the world at large reaped the benefit of their sufferings. Thus God overrules all things to work out his will. The record of the Spaniards in America is a dark one. They treated the Indians with miserable cruelty, enticed them on their vessels, and carried them away into slavery. One of their last acts was the massacre of a colony of Huguenots, who were French Protestants and had settled in Florida. They planted a colony of Catholics in its place, and called it St. Augustine. This is the oldest town in the United States by forty years, but it was founded in cruelty and bigotry, and never flourished. Indeed, the Spaniards had no success in any attempt to plant settlements on the soil of the United States, for God had reserved this territory to be settled by Protestants."

"What a merciful Providence!" exclaimed Nannie. "Those dreadful Spaniards might have brought the cruel Inquisition into our beautiful country."

"Yes, merciful indeed," continued Aunt Edith; "but God was preparing better things for this favored land and for his chosen people, even a Gospel of love and not of hate, of 'peace on earth and good-will to men.' Such spirits as George Fox, Hooker, and Roger Williams, John Wesley, Whitefield, and Jonathan Edwards were to be the spiritual Fathers and the heralds of this Gospel of love to the dwellers in the New World. In all the history of the race I know of no more visible manifestation of divine interference than the early annals of our country afford: God making 'bare his arm in the eyes of all the people.' Again and again, as I read the record of his providential arrangements, I recall the words of inspiration, 'What could have been done more to my vineyard that I have not done in it?' And, dear children, you are not too young to realize the great responsibility that rests upon you, and upon all the children of this Christian land, and to understand something of the import of those solemn words, 'Where much is given much shall be required!' But now let me tell you something about Sir Walter Raleigh and his brother.

"The English made many unsuccessful attempts at colonization before they finally took

root in the New World.   The efforts made by
Sir Humphrey Gilbert and Sir Walter Raleigh
were the most interesting because of the character of these men.   They were two English
Protestant noblemen, noble both by nature and
by birth.   They were step-brothers.   They obtained a patent from Queen Elizabeth, and fitted out two expeditions, spending much of their
private fortunes in aid of them.   Gilbert was a
man of great piety.   He braved danger without
fear, because 'he knew that death was inevitable, and the fame of virtue immortal.'   The
first expedition failed ; part of the ships were
scattered and lost in fierce storms, others were
turned back, the men being terrified by suffering and privation.

   "Gilbert returned home and fitted out another expedition, but the elements were not
more kind than before.   His largest vessels were
wrecked, some others deserted to become pi-
rates, and he was again obliged to return homeward.   They encountered 'outrageous storms.'
The vessel in which Gilbert sailed was named
the 'Squirrel,' a small frail vessel.   The brave
man, sitting calmly at the helm, cried out to
the terrified seamen, 'We are as near to heav-
en by sea as by land.'   At midnight the lights
of the 'Squirrel' suddenly disappeared, and as

brave a heart as ever beat was swallowed up in the great deep.

"Sir Walter Raleigh was not discouraged by the sad fate of his brother, but he continued to encourage emigration to America, for he foresaw that one day a great nation would people it. He spent a princely fortune in fitting out expeditions, and twice planted colonies in Roanoke Island, North Carolina. The settlers of the first colony grew homesick in these faraway wilds, and went back to England. The others perished for want of provisions.

"Sir Walter Raleigh was not only a skillful sailor and an experienced soldier, but he was also an accomplished scholar and a graceful courtier—a very prince among men. He served England for years in her navy, served God and the human race by fighting bravely in the cause of Protestantism when it was assailed by Catholicism, and served the cause of science and knowledge by traveling, exploring, and collecting valuable information. Yet an ungrateful king—James I., a man of essentially mean nature—suffered him to languish in prison for years on a false charge, and at last consented to his execution. This man in his old age ascended, with palsied limbs that could scarcely support him, an English scaffold, and was beheaded. But his enemies could not consign his name to silence, for, two centuries afterward, the State of North Carolina gave to her capital city the name of 'Raleigh,' thus expressing their affection for one of the most extraordinary men who ever lived."

"Why, aunty, his story is sadder than that of Columbus," said Albert, gravely.

"And I like him just as well," added Nannie; "don't you, Aunt Edith."

"I confess, children, the history of all these heroic men, the early discoverers and explorers of our country, awakened in me the greatest admiration. They embarked on these expeditions in frail vessels, that none of us would be brave enough to venture to sea in to-day. They knew nothing of tides and currents, as we do. So great was the risk that the crews used to engage in solemn acts of devotion before starting. Disaster, suffering, and death they met without a murmur. Terrific storms washed them down into watery graves; the beautiful but cruel icebergs of our northern coasts inclosed them in icy arms to frozen tombs; they sickened with fevers peculiar to strange climates, and filled lonely graves far from home; or, escaping from these perils, they returned home to meet the still more cruel arrows of malice and envy from the hands of false friends or ungrateful patrons. Yet, nothing daunted, they pursued their way, moved by a lofty ambition to increase human knowledge and become the benefactors of their race. They labored, and those who came after entered into their labors."

Here Harry gave a low growl, which being interpreted meant that he was glad we had no kings in this country.

CHAPTER III.

Virginia Colonized—John Smith. Maryland Colonized—Lord Baltimore.

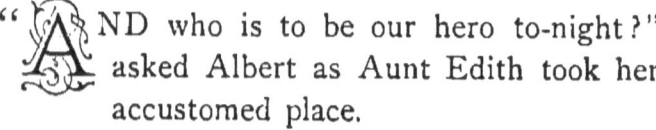 "AND who is to be our hero to-night?" asked Albert as Aunt Edith took her accustomed place.

"John Smith," replied Aunt Edith.

"Ah! I think I have heard that name before," said Albert, smiling.

"You are joking, aunty," said Harry.

"Not at all, my boy; only wait until you know him, and I think you will find enough of romance and heroism in his life and character to lend a halo to every descendant of the immortal race of John Smiths. This John Smith was the father of English colonization in the United States."

"Let him come in at once," said Harry, drawing up a large arm-chair toward the table, "he shall have the best seat in the room."

"Not quite yet, if you please," returned Aunt Edith; "where did our story break off last night?"

"With Sir Walter Raleigh and his North Carolina colonies, in 1590," answered Nannie.

" How long since the discovery in 1492 ?"

" Just ninety-eight years."

" Quite right, Nannie. Now notice, children, almost a hundred years had passed in what might seem at first sight to be failures—vain attempts to colonize North America. Much money and many valuable lives had certainly been given to it. True, these colonies had not yet taken root ; but very much had been accomplished by the visits and explorations of Europeans to this continent. The study of history convinces us that Providence works slowly—' Making no haste, taking no rest.' Our heroes of last evening, with others whom we could not take time to tell of, had accomplished much. The Cabots had discovered North America under English patent. Cabeza de Vacca and Ferdinand de Soto had penetrated the interior and mighty West. Gilbert and Raleigh had explored and written the history of the fairest portions of the eastern coast, which they named Virginia, in honor of the virgin Queen Elizabeth. They had described its noble rivers, its safe and commodious harbors, its fertile soil and varied productions, and it was pronounced 'the goodliest soil under the cope of heaven. If Virginia had but horses and kine, and were inhabited with

English, no realm in Chrisfendom were com-
parable to it.'

"Ship-load after ship-load of useless dirt had
been carried back to Europe, and the people
had waked up out of their dream of gold hunt-
ing and getting suddenly and lazily rich. They
saw now clearly that the riches were there, but
only as the reward of patient toil. The idea
now was to people this excellent country with
English, establish commercial relations with
the settlers, and so both the colonies and the
mother country would be benefited and enriched. With this view, the next attempt to
plant a colony in Virginia was made by a company of London merchants and business men.
John Smith, our hero, was one of the leading
spirits of this expedition. His whole previous
life seemed a preparation for it. Though he
was not yet thirty years old, his history was a
catalogue of romantic adventures and brave
exploits. In boyhood he had left England to
battle for the cause of religious freedom in Holland. Afterward he roamed through Europe
and crossed the Mediterranean into Egypt;
returning thence, he joined the Christians in
Hungary, and helped to beat back the Mo-
hammedans. Many and many a Turk went
down before him in single combat, until his

comrades thought he bore a charmed life, and wielded a charmed sword, and the Turks feared him, and fled from him as an avenging spirit. At length, with a few others, being overpowered in a skirmish on the battle-field, he fell dangerously wounded. He was now a prisoner of war, sold like a beast in the market-place, and sent to Constantinople as a slave. The extreme youth and noble appearance of the young English captive excited the interest of a Turkish lady, and by her assistance he escaped from bondage. He wandered in disguise through pathless forests, and once was on the point of perishing of hunger, when the hand of woman again rescued him and sent him on his way. He had resolved now to return to his own 'sweet country,' but on his way he heard of the breaking out of civil war in North Africa. The martial spirit got the mastery, and he hastened to win fresh glory in this far-off clime. At length he turned his steps to the home of his youth, 'dear England.' He arrived just in time to enter with all the enthusiasm of his nature into the scheme of colonizing the New World.

"The little company embarked on three vessels, December 19, 1606. As they neared the coast of Virginia a storm arose and drove them into the 'magnificent bay of Chesapeake.'

Passing the Capes at its mouth, which they called Charles and Henry, after the king's two sons—Albert, find them on your map—they entered a noble river, which they named James, after the king, and sailing up the stream about fifty miles they anchored, selected a site, and called it Jamestown.   Their troubles soon came, sickness first, then quarrels among themselves and with their president, who was a selfish, money-loving man, and looked for his own interest only.   This had nearly caused the breaking up of the colony, which was only prevented by dismissing him and putting John Smith at the head of affairs.   Then cheerfulness succeeded to gloom, and hope animated every heart.   Smith knew human nature under all its forms.   His genius and resolute will made him a leader, a master, wherever he was.   Men obeyed him because they could not resist him.   He soon subdued the spirit of disorder among the colonists, and inspired the Indians with awe and submission.   But Smith's discerning eye saw that the great difficulty in the way of the success of the colony was the character of the colonists themselves.   There were too many useless gentlemen in their little community, who were willing to eat while others planted, and enjoy themselves while others labored.

Smith saw that honest, industrious laboring men, with wives and families, were the right class for immigrants to a new country. He wrote back to England to the London Company, 'When you send again, I entreat you, send rather thirty carpenters, gardeners, fishermen, and blacksmiths, than a thousand such as we now have.'

"In the fall Smith left the colony in a good condition, and taking a few men he started to explore the coasts of the Chesapeake Bay. Through disobedience to his orders they were captured by a party of hostile Indians. They put all but Smith to instant death ; his courage and self-possession overpowered them. He had a mysterious power of bringing men under his control. He was conducted, with a sort of awe and reverence mixed with fear, from settlement to settlement. They did not know what to do with him. They feared him alive, and were still more afraid to kill him, for they thought him more than man. He was a great trouble to them. Again and again in their councils it was decided to put him to death, and as often it was delayed for fear of the evil his spirit might do them. At last a grand council was called, and his death once more decided. He was led out and the tomahawk raised to sever his head, when, for the third time in his history, a woman interfered and rescued him. Smith had won the heart of the youthful Indian maiden Pocahontas, daughter of the chief Powhattan, and the pride of her tribe for beauty and intelligence. She threw herself upon Smith's neck, and would not relinquish her hold until her father promised to spare his life. He returned to the colony to find it relapsed into a state of confusion and weakness. The only wish of the colonists was to quit the country and return to England. They were not brave enough to endure its hardships. But Smith forbade it, and resisted their purpose at the hazard of his own life.

" While he struggled to keep the colony from being thus uprooted, a vessel arrived with more immigrants and provisions, and they all resumed their work of planting crops and building houses. Unfortunately an accidental explosion of gunpowder wounded Smith so severely that he was obliged to resign his position and return to England. Intense bodily suffering and the ingratitude of his employers were all that Smith earned for his great service to the colony. ' Not one foot of land,' says the historian, 'not the house his own hands had built, nor the field his own hands had planted, nor any reward but the

applause of his own conscience and the world
He was the father of Virginia, and the true
leader who first planted the English race in the
United States.' Many times his courage and
genius saved the colony from utter failure. He
sent home the most glowing accounts of the
country he had explored, and urged them to
hasten over reinforcements ; for a feeble colony
in a new country is like a new-born infant, and
requires constant feeding. He held it up as
one would a feeble child until its limbs were
strong enough to support it. His interest did
not flag when he returned to England. He carried back correct and valuable maps of Virginia
and Maryland, made from his own observations,
and stimulated emigration to America more
than any other one man. He was as generous
of soul as he was brave of spirit, and as hand-
some as he was brave. Here, I have a picture
of him."

The children crowded round to look at the
brave adventurer. All begged for it, but it was
finally awarded to Stevey.

"Tell us more about him, aunty," exclaimed
Harry ; "please, don't stop ; didn't he get well
of his wounds and come back to America ?"

Aunt Edith smiled and shook her head, saying, "We must hasten on, children. There are

4

other heroes waiting their turn, and I want to tell you something about the settlement of Maryland.

"Sir George Calvert, Lord Baltimore, was an English nobleman of high rank. He had watched with the greatest interest the progress of the colonies in America, and had done much to promote their success. While he was a man of much learning and great wisdom as a statesman, he was also one of the purest spirits of his age. His life bloomed with beautiful deeds, which sprung from the stock of gentlest Christian virtues. He was a devout Catholic, not by birth, but by conviction. England was now a Protestant country, and Protestantism also must own to its persecutions. Calvert was too candid to conceal his opinions; he openly professed Catholicism, and resigned his high position at court with all its advantages. But he continued to be a great favorite with King Charles; and as the controversies between Catholics and Protestants became more and more bitter, the gentle Calvert projected in his mind a quiet asylum in the forests of the New World, where the strife of religious disputes should never be heard, and where Protestant and Catholic should be alike protected in their right to worship God as they thought best. King

James was now dead, and King Charles, his son, reigned in England."

" I hope he was a better man than his father," exclaimed Nannie ; " I shall always think of King James as the man who took Sir Walter Raleigh's head off."

Aunt Edith was very patient with the children's interruptions if they related to the story in any way. She added, " I will give you a rhyme in this connection ; you may repeat it after me.

> ' Our acts our angels are, or good or ill,
> Our fatal shadows that walk by us still.'

" This King Charles was a weak, vain, foolish man, who excites our pity more perhaps than any other feeling. There had been English kings more wicked than he, but by his weakness and ignorance he brought great trouble upon England, and at the last they took off his head. He belonged to the unfortunate race of Stuarts, descendants of the ill-fated Mary, Queen of Scots, who herself died upon the scaffold. It was a weak race ; they were wanting in moral principle, and had no capacity to rule. Charles thought more of his own pleasure and comfort than any thing else, and cared little for what was taking place in the forests of America. Besides, Calvert was a favorite at court, and when he applied for a grant of territory in that far-off land he readily obtained it. The territory was given to Lord Baltimore and his heirs forever; it was to be free from English taxation, and the settlers were allowed to make their own laws. It was the most generous grant of liberties that had ever been obtained by emigrants, for Sir George was a far-seeing man, and had observed how the laws and restrictions on other colonies had burdened them and hindered their success. When all was prepared, and the good Sir George was about to sail with his company, death came and took him a longer journey, and, without doubt, to a better country; but his son succceded to all his father's claims in America, and most worthily he carried out his father's plans, at vast expense, from his own private purse. They sailed from England in November, 1633, about two hundred Catholic gentlemen and their families and servants, in two vessels, the 'Ark' and the 'Dove.' They ascended the Potomac in March, 1634, planted a cross, and claimed the country for Christ and England. The spot was nearly opposite Mount Vernon, where now lies the sacred dust of the 'Father of his Country.' They gave presents to the Indians and asked their friendship. The Indians made a treaty

of peace with the white men, and shared their
provision with them. The squaws taught the
wives of the English how to make bread of
maize, and the Indian warriors joined the English in the chase, and taught them how to en-
trap the game of the forests. They also gave
them their ʾhuts to shelter them until their
houses were ready."

"Why, how pleasant it must have been,
aunty!" cried little Stevey; "so much better
than to be cruel and make enemies of the poor
Indians."

"Yes, indeed, my darling Stevey; if all the
immigrants, from their first coming among the
Indians, had been just and kind, it would have
saved much of the blood that years after flowed
in such profusion, and would have prevented
the horrible cruelties that make us shudder to
think of. The foundations of this colony were
laid in peace, and truth, and happiness, and in
six months it flourished more than Virginia had
in six years. The colonists could buy grain
and cattle from Virginia, and were in no fear
of hunger. They were well governed, for they
governed themselves. There was no interference from England, and Lord Calvert provided
at his own expense whatever was needed for
their comfort and prosperity. Under his mild

and kind laws the wilderness soon bloomed with life and industry. Catholics, oppressed at home, found here a peaceful refuge, and Protestants, too, could worship as their conscience bid them. The governor was obliged to take an oath that he 'would not directly nor indirectly molest any person, professing to believe in Jesus Christ, for or in respect of religion.' 'The country,' says a historian, 'was dear to its inhabitants; there they desired to spend the remnant of their lives; there they covenanted to make their graves.'"

"That is a pleasant picture of forest life, aunty," said Albert. "I hope our fathers will have it more agreeable as we go on."

"I will not anticipate," returned Aunt Edith, "only to say, that as their day was, so was their strength."

CHAPTER IV.

Massachusetts Colonized—Pilgrims—Sir Harry Vane.

ATTLEDOOR and shuttlecock, ball and grace hoops, were all away in their places, and the children in their seats, waiting for Aunt Edith and the hero of the evening. Aunt Edith was punctual to the hour, saying, as she seated herself at the table, "I think I have thus far fulfilled my promise, children, to give you at least one new hero each evening, but to-night 'their name is legion.'"

"O, aunty, I guess I know who they are!" exclaimed Nannie.

"Who?" asked Harry, looking blank.

"I know, I know," repeated Nannie.

No light beamed from either of the boys' faces, and Aunt Edith and Steve exchanged winks.

"You've been peeping into Aunt Edith's portfolio to-day," said Harry; "that's the way you've got the start of us."

"Not I, indeed,' replied Nannie. "Aunty keeps her portfolio locked."

"Well, if you have any wisdom that we

haven't," said Albert, "please let us have it at once, and get on with the story."

"You had better be sure you're right before you go ahead," suggested Harry.

"Well, I am sure I am right. You are going to tell us about the Pilgrim Fathers, aunty."

"O, bother! why didn't I think of them," said Harry, scratching his head.

"'Most potent, grave, and reverend seigneurs,'" said Albert; "I think I see them in my mind's eye with their steeple hats and broad ruffs."

"Well, let 'em come in," said Harry. "How many are there? if there are not chairs enough," looking round the room, "I'll fetch some more."

"Before they come in," said Aunt Edith, "I would like to hear, Albert, what you remember of last evening's story."

"The first permanent English settlement in this country, at Jamestown, Virginia, 1606, by John Smith."

"Very well answered. What do you remember, Harry?"

"The settlement of Maryland, by Sir George Calvert, in 1634."

"Very well; what does Albert mean by 'permanent,' Stevey?" said Aunt Edith, stroking back the curls from the little thoughtful face.

"He means that—that—well, they stayed here and did not go back home, as the others had done."

"Yes, that's it, my little Steve. They took firm hold of the soil, and grew and flourished. We shall have to go back a little in point of time. Our Pilgrim Fathers anchored at Plymouth Rock, December, 1620—fourteen years after the Jamestown settlement, and fourteen years before the settlement of Maryland. I placed the story of the Virginia and Maryland colonies together because they were such near neighbors, and their history has always been intimately associated. Before our Pilgrims land I want to tell you something about their history in their own country. Since the date of Columbus' discovery of this Western World, great changes had taken place in Europe both in religion and in government. The art of printing had made books more abundant, and people were better informed. They saw that the old systems of religion and government needed reformation. In England the authority of the Pope was set aside, and King Henry VIII. declared himself head of the English Church. But the good Martin Luther, in Germany, had overthrown the authority of the pope, and declared that God was the only true head of the Church, and that all men had the right to worship him, without the intervention of pope, or priest, or king, or any other man. Luther had many followers in England, who, in matters of religion, did not want to obey the king any more than the pope. These were called Dissenters, and were Presbyterians, Quakers, and Puritans. Our Pilgrim Fathers were Puritans ; they wanted 'a Church without a bishop, and a State without a king.' They wanted only a pure Gospel and the simplest form of worship. They did not wish to use the written service of the Church of England, nor to listen to their printed prayers, nor submit to the authority of their haughty bishops. King James was very bitter against them. He said they should conform to the prayer-book, and all the rules of the Church, or he would 'harry them out of the land.' He thought to conquer them and break their spirit, but he could not. They refused to worship in the churches, or use their prayers. They met for worship in their own houses ; sometimes in the forests or in caves and dens. But they were hunted out. They were whipped and put in stocks ; they had their heads shaved, and their ears cut off, and some were brought to the stake and nobly suffered death rather than yield the truth that every man has a right to worship

God according to his own conscience, and in the way he thinks best. This treatment, instead of curing them of their folly, as the king and the bishops thought it would, or discouraging others from joining them, only made them more powerful. At last the king made a decree that they should either come to his church, and pray as he prayed, or else they should be driven out of the kingdom. Would they yield? No. There is a rare element of courage in the English character, which, when it is roused on the side of right, is sublime. They turned their backs on their homes and their worldly possessions, and taking their wives and little ones they became strangers and pilgrims in foreign lands. A large number, led by their pastor, the good and great John Robinson, passed over the sea to Holland.

" Here they had rest for their souls, but they were not happy. The country was strange ; the people and the language were not theirs. In England they had been farmers ; here they were obliged to learn new trades, or find some employment to make their bread. They were very poor and suffered much, yet they did not wish to return to England. But often they talked together of the goodly land across the sea, and their hearts longed for a quiet habita-

tion in the wilderness, where they could sit unmolested under 'their own vine and fig-tree.'
Notwithstanding the persecutions of the king
their English hearts still clung to their own
land, and if they planted a colony in America
they felt they would be under the patronage of
England. But would King James grant them
a charter, securing to them the rights of English
subjects, and yet leave them their religious privileges? They sent over petitioners from Holland to ask this favor of the king, but the king
was gruff. He referred them to the bishops;
they were not less so. Nothing more could be
obtained than 'a promise of neglect.' They
were thankful to get that, and the Pilgrims resolved to go to America without a charter, or
patent, or king's seal, 'for,' said they among
themselves, 'if there should be afterward a purpose to wrong us, though we had a seal as
broad as the house-floor, there would be means
found to recall or break it.' But they were
very poor, and had no way of getting across the
ocean to their new home. After casting the
subject about in their minds, and praying much
to God for direction, they entered into an agree-
ment with some London merchants, who were
to pay all their expenses across the ocean, and
the Pilgrims were to give them an interest in

the profits of their crops, fisheries, and all their labors for the first seven years after they reached America.

"So the youngest and strongest made ready to go over first, with their wives and little ones. Before their departure they appointed a day of solemn fast, for the Pilgrims began all their enterprises with prayer. The whole congregation assembled, 'and,' says one of them, 'we refreshed ourselves with tears and the singing of psalms, making joyful melody in our hearts, and indeed it was the sweetest melody that ever mine ears heard. Afterward those that remained feasted us, and then accompanied us unto the ship, when a flood of tears was poured out, and we were not able to speak to one another for the abundance of sorrow; so lifting up our hands to each other and our hearts for each other unto the Lord, we departed.' Two vessels, the 'Speedwell' and the 'Mayflower,' carried the little company, but, after some days out, the 'Speedwell' was obliged to put back as unseaworthy. The 'Mayflower' held on her course, freighted with her one hundred and two souls, and after a long and perilous voyage they found themselves, in the month of December, on the chill, barren coast of New England, for so they fondly called it, with the ocean behind them, the wilderness before them, and no friendly voice to bid them welcome. They beat about the coast some time to discover a favorable landing-place. Says one of them, 'It snowed, and did blow all the day, and froze withal. The spray of the sea froze as it fell on us and made our garments like coats of iron.' At length they found safe harbor on the coast of Massachusetts, cast anchor fast by Plymouth Rock, and sang a hymn of thanksgiving.* The voyage had been much longer than they had expected ; their provisions were nearly exhausted ; this, added to the severity of the season, brought suffering, wasting disease, and death to thin out their numbers. They made what haste they could to put up houses, but snow and rain and freezing cold interrupted their work, and many died from lung-fevers and rapid consumptions."

"What a pity they came in the winter !" said little Stevey.

"O dear, yes ! and why did they go so far north in that bleak country," said Nannie. "They ought to have gone to Maryland."

"Maryland wasn't settled yet," said Harry with a wise wink.

"Well, they talked all that over, and prayed

* See Frontispiece.

over it too, children. They knew it would have
been far easier and more comfortable for them
to go to the Virginia settlements, but you must
keep in view the object of their coming. It was
to enjoy their special form of religious worship.
Now Virginia was settled under the king's
charter, and the Church of England was to be
the established Church in the colony. After
the settlement of Maryland, the good Calvert
sent them a cordial invitation to leave the
rocky shores of New England, and cast in their
lot with his colony in the mild and genial climate of Maryland, where religious liberty was
granted to all. But the Pilgrims would not go.
They preferred their rocky, ice-bound homes
in the far north, if they might only keep their
pure and simple forms of worship, and so have a
conscience void of offense. They did not want
people of any other faith to settle with them,
lest disputes and dissensions should arise. In
the midst of all their sufferings, and on their
dying beds, their faith supported them, they
rejoiced 'in hope of a better country, even a
heavenly,' and died without a regret that they
had left all to follow the light God had given
them. Amid poverty and suffering, beyond any
thing I can relate, they triumphed with a 'joy
unspeakable;' feeling that though they were out-

casts from their earthly homes, they were 'kings and priests' to the living God, and exhorted those they left behind to hold fast their confidence and stand up valiantly for the truth.

"Winter wore away. Spring came, and brought with it sweet south winds and the song of birds. The trees opened their thousand leaves of tender green, and the woods were full of the scent of wild flowers, vines, and pleasant fruits. Disease and death disappeared from among them, their houses were now up, and busy hands were planting and cultivating the earth. Their hearts were filled with hope, and their souls with peace. After the labors of the day they assembled to worship God, and their songs and hymns of praise made the forests echo. They thanked God for the goodly heritage he had given them ; they loved their wildwood homes, and hoped only to live and die here unmolested by kings or bishops. They called themselves loyal subjects of England, and many a prayer went up for 'dear England,' though they were still very glad to be three thousand miles away from her. They governed themselves. In all matters of law they came together in a body, for they were yet but few, and decided their own questions. Their ministers were their magistrates, and they called themselves a Church in the wilderness. They sent back words of cheer to their friends in England, who were still persecuted for conscience' sake, and advised them to follow them to the wilderness, for it was surely God's hand that had led them thither, and he would raise up a great nation to his honor and praise. The oppressed people heard and received it as a call from God, and they came. Ship after ship discharged on the shores of Massachusetts its precious freight of noble souls. Settlements sprang up as if by magic all through the wilderness. Far into the interior, and down the beautiful valley of the Connecticut River, the immigrants pushed their way, driving their flocks before them, their wives and little ones with them. The Indians were very friendly to the early settlers, sold them lands, and made treaties of peace with them. They flourished and prospered. Comfortable dwelling-houses were built, then the churches, and soon the school-houses followed. In a few years thousands of English Dissenters had passed over the sea and made their homes in the Western World. Many of them were people of noble birth, great intelligence, and ample wealth.

"With this tide of population that poured into the flourishing New England settlements,

many came who were not of their faith. This
was a grief to the early Puritans, because they
had forsaken all to possess this little corner of
the earth where they could be safe from disputes and controversies ; but they expected too
much, for it is impossible for even good people
to see eye to eye. The Puritans, we are sorry
to record it, persecuted some who came among
them ; then they banished them from the colony,
and it would have been better if they had remained away or gone to some other part of
America, seeing there was abundance of room
for all, but they would not. They came back
and troubled them so much that at last the
sturdy old Puritan magistrates had several of
them hung as examples, declaring, however,
that 'we desired their lives absent rather than
their deaths present.'

"It is a grief to me to tell you this, children,
but candor compels me. Perfection we cannot
find in any thing human ; it belongs not to
man nor to any of his works. Our virtues and
our religion are all tainted with human infirmity. The enemies of the Puritans are fond of
charging them with intolerance and persecutions, but it ought to be remembered that the
spirit of persecution was the spirit of that age.
We must judge the past by its own light, not

by ours in this better day. All sects and civil authorities persecuted those who differed from them, and the Puritans did less of it than any other people, except the Quakers. Besides, many of the Puritans themselves had risen above these narrow views, and were true followers of the great and good John Robinson, who led them out of England into Holland, but was too old and feeble to come with them to America. When they embarked on the 'Mayflower' he gave them a sublime charge: that they should not think they possessed the whole truth and had nothing more to learn. He told them the Lord had 'more truth yet to break forth out of his holy word,' and they must be willing to receive it with all humility. Among his followers were two young ministers of holy lives and 'precious gifts,' Roger Williams and Hooker, who went through the colonies preaching these sublime and glorious doctrines and winning many to their views. They declared it a sin to persecute any man for any religious opinion, and that truth would always be strong enough to overcome error without the aid of physical force.

"Puritanism may lift its head without fear, graced with such names as Roger Williams, Winthrop, Hooker, and a host of others more

than I have time to mention, though I must tell
you of one, as noble a hero as ever sealed his
truth with his blood. I mean the good Sir
Harry Vane. He had been at one time governor of Massachusetts, but returned to England
to plead the cause of the Puritans who were
still persecuted there, and not alone their cause,
but that of all who were wronged for religious
opinions, whether it were Catholic, Puritan,
Presbyterian, or Quaker. He was a man of
great gifts and eloquence, and had such weight
with the people that his enemies at last resolved
to take his life. As you study history you will
find, children, that those who are in error, when
they find themselves out-argued and about to
lose their cause, always resort to brute force.
If they cannot kill the truth, they will try to kill
the man who utters it. King Charles was persuaded that he ought to bring him to the block.
But Sir Harry Vane went to the scaffold as
calmly as he would have gone to his bed. The
people followed him in throngs, weeping and
blessing him who had been the friend of his
race ; not of his party, nor his sect, nor his
class only, but of all mankind. He would have
spoken to the poor weeping people, but his
enemies would not let him, for they were afraid
of the great and precious truths that fell from

his lips, so they drowned his voice with the sound of their trumpets. But they could not take the glory and beauty out of his countenance, and the people 'saw his face as it had been the face of an angel.' He kissed and embraced his dear little children, and bade them not be troubled, for God would be a father to them. Thus he died with his soul full of peace, and in strong faith that though *he* died the truth would live. It does live ; the liberties we enjoy in our dear country this day are the fruits of that truth. So we will bless and honor our Pilgrim Fathers for all they suffered and wrought for us."

As Aunt Edith stopped speaking, Harry brought his fist down upon the table with such a noise as made all the children jump, and exclaimed, " Blast 'em, I hate kings ! "

Steve buried his face on Aunt Edith's shoulder, and cried outright to think of the dear little children who had to lose so good a father. Aunt Edith comforted him, and bade him not to cry, saying, " It is all over now ; it was a quick, short way up to the heavenly Father's house, whither the noble army of martyrs are gathering out of all the ages.

" Sir Harry Vane made a glorious end, and his life and his death equally blessed the world.

Remember, dear children, that in the eternal councils there stands the sure word, continually being fulfilled, 'without the shedding of blood there is no remission of sin ;' and as the ages come and go, God's holy martyrs attest it with their lives, and thus, in their human measure, fill up that which is behind of the sufferings of their divine Master.

"Let us also seek after this same spirit, children, so shall we be ready, at God's command, to 'resist unto blood, striving against sin.'"

CHAPTER V. ·

Pennsylvania Colonized—William Penn.

" PEN your maps, children, and trace our colonies as they creep along the coast of North America. We have Virginia and Maryland settled from the James River to the Chesapeake Bay. Our Pilgrim Fathers have dotted all the country from the Connecticut to the Penobscot rivers with happy, prosperous settlements, and called it New England.

"The Dutch had been the first to explore what we now know as New York. They had penetrated into the interior, and ascended the beautiful Hudson River as far as Albany. They also planted a colony on Manhattan Island, where the metropolis of the Western World now stands, our magnificent city of New York ; and they called the few Dutch hamlets that then composed the city, New Amsterdam.

"The Dutch were a great commercial people at that time, and their vessels whitened every sea and ocean of the world. They foresaw what a great city would one day rise on this spot. The Dutch settlement grew very rapidly in wealth, and brought much profit to the company of merchants who lived in Holland and controlled its affairs. Their great object was to make money, and in this they succeeded; but when a war broke out between England and Holland, England sent a fleet to New Amsterdam, and took possession of the city and all the territory which they had settled. She added it to her other American colonies, and the name of the city was changed from New Amsterdam to New York, in compliment to the king's brother, the Duke of York. A little further down the coast the lands were settled by a colony of Swedish Protestants, under the protection of the great and good king Gustavus Adolphus. Harry, you look surprised to hear me call a king great and good. There have been many such. When you come to know them and their good works you will perhaps think better of kings. This good king, when the German Protestants were threatened with being overwhelmed by the Catholics, and the principles of religious liberty were in danger of being destroyed by fire and sword, left his throne and his kingdom and led a noble army to the defense of the right cause. In a great and decisive battle he fell, bravely fighting, but his army won the victory, and truth triumphed.

After his death the Swedish colonies in America languished, for they missed his care and wisdom ; and in course of time they mingled with the English colonists around them, and became one with them."

" Is Gustavus our hero this evening ?" asked Albert.

" No, Albert, although he was a true hero ; but I want to tell you about the Quaker settlements on the left bank of the Delaware, and the founding of the colony of Pennsylvania and the city of Philadelphia by William Penn."

" What ! a Quaker hero ?" asked Nannie, despairingly.

" Yes, verily, Nannie, a Quaker hero," answered Aunt Edith, holding up a picture of the young reformer, in the dress of an English cavalier, with flowing curls over his shoulders, and a face of womanly tenderness and beauty.

" O, is that William Penn ?" asked Nannie, brightening up. " I thought he would have his hair smoothed off behind his ears, under a broad-brimmed hat, with a long yellow coat like Uncle Jesse's."

" I should take him for a poet, aunty," said Albert.

" So he was, Albert, of the highest order— his life was a poem ; good deeds are better than

good words. The founder of Quakerism was
George Fox, son of a poor English weaver, but
so good a man that he was called 'righteous
Christopher!' His mother was descended from
the stock of martyrs. Little George was first
apprenticed to a shoemaker, and afterward to a
farmer, and he watched the sheep like King
David of old. He liked keeping the sheep; it
gave him time to dream—I mean with his eyes
open—and think and pray, for he was a praying
boy. But the more he wept and prayed and
struggled, the more miserable and bewildered
he was. He could not understand those strange,
mysterious things, life and death, God and his
own soul, nor be satisfied exactly as to what his
duty was. His parents belonged to the English
Church, but he found no rest there; he went
among the Dissenters—the Puritans and Presbyterians—but all to no purpose. They could
not show him 'the path of life.'

"Whole days and nights he spent in agony
of prayer, until one day, sitting in deep thought
by the winter's fire, he heard a voice in his own
soul. It was not audible to the outward ear;
it was 'a still, small voice' that only the spirit's
ear could hear. This voice told him that God
was not in any Church, or council, or creed, or
with any priest or bishop, or in any temple

made with human hands ; but he was in every
human soul, and if they would but listen none
need go astray, for God would teach them by
his Spirit what they must do to be saved.   He
called it the 'inner light,' which was, verily,
'God in the soul.'   It was also in every man's
soul, for God was no respecter of persons ; so,
of course, all men of every race and name were
equal before him.   One was not above another,
except as there was more faithfulness in walk-
ing by the 'inner light.'   Now, this was thought
by many to be a very wicked and shameful
doctrine.   Where were the kings, with their
crowns and royal robes?   Where were the
nobles and mighty men?   Where were the
priests and bishops of the true Church?   Were
they indeed no better than this poor man, the
weaver's son, wasted and worn by his prayers
and watchings, and meanly dressed in leathern
breeches?   And the poor rabble that followed
him were only cowherds, shoemakers, and the
like.   'No, verily,' answered Fox, 'no better.'
So he would call no man king or lord, save only
him who was 'King of kings and Lord of lords.'
The followers of Fox said naught to any man
but 'thee and thou,' and refused to lift their
hats to any, for they said, 'the Lord forbade it.'
Now, lest you might think that this was a

foolish thing for the Quakers to refuse to do,
I must explain that it meant more than you
might suppose. It was the custom of that day
for the highest nobility to keep their hats on in
the presence of the king, to denote that they
were his equals. Those of lower rank were not
permitted to come into the king's presence with
their heads covered. To uncover the head always signified inferiority. The Quaker creed
declared all men equal, therefore they would
not uncover their heads to any man, though
they would love and serve all men as brothers
and equals. As you may suppose, such a doctrine made the great men and the worldly
wise men exceedingly mad. They beat honest
George Fox and put him into prison, but he
employed the time in praying and communing
with God, and after awhile when they released
him he preached only the more powerfully.
The people thronged in crowds to hear him,
and his prayers were so filled with life and
spirit that it seemed as if the very heavens
opened to his call. Of course, he made a great
many believe as he did, and among those who
were converted to the new doctrines was our
hero, William Penn.

" Penn was of noble birth, the son of a brave
officer in the English navy, who had a great

name at court for his gallant services to his
country. William was his only son, and while
he was yet at college, only seventeen years old,
he heard one of these wandering Quaker preach-
ers. His heart was stirred within him. He
could never pray 'by the book' afterward. This
was the rule at the college, so they fined him,
and as he still refused, saying that God had
taught him 'a more excellent way,' they ex-
pelled him. This was a heavy trial to the young
ambitious student. But his trials were worse
when he reached home, for his father was so
enraged to think that his only son, the son of a
noble house, would disgrace himself by going
with such low people as the Quakers, that he
whipped him and turned him from his door,
thinking by this prompt treatment to bring him
to his senses. His mother interceded for him,
and his father gave him money, and sent him
to travel in Europe, to divert his mind from his
foolishness. Penn was a serious, observing traveler. While in France he studied the history
of the people called Huguenots—I shall tell
you more about them another time—and having gathered much wisdom by his travels, he
returned to England. He is described, at this
time; as most engaging and pleasing in manner
and appearance, skillful in speech and debate,

every way calculated to adorn the court of the king, and with every prospect of advancement, because of the high favor in which his father was held. But, alas! for this father's ambitious plans for his gifted son. Penn found his heart still drawn to that simple people called Quakers, and, while listening to one of them explaining 'the faith that overcometh the world' he embraced the doctrine, received the faith in his own heart, and, like Moses of old, refused the treasures of the king's court, choosing rather to suffer affliction with God's people. Thus beautifully he tells us of it: 'Into that path God in his everlasting kindness guided my feet in the flower of my youth, when about two and twenty years of age.'

"He was mocked and scorned by his family and friends, and it was told as a good joke that William Penn had turned Quaker, and his father had driven him without a penny from his door. You see, children, what Penn's principles cost him. His was no easy virtue. He could not possibly have borne all this except by that faith that overcomes the world and all that it contains. He was very brave. He went at once to court with his hat on to plead with the king and his ministers to allow the English people freedom of conscience, so that they might worship God as they saw best, and prayed him to let the Quakers out of the stocks and prisons where hundreds of them were now confined. They laughed at him, and handed him over to my Lord Bishop of London, and he sent him to the Tower, a prison where they put criminals of high rank. King Charles, however, did not like Penn to be shut up in the Tower, because of his brave father who had done such service to his country, and he sent another bishop to persuade Penn to give up his strange doctrines, and come out and behave like other young English noblemen. Penn sent word back to the king that the Tower was the worst argument in the world, and he continued from his prison to proclaim his principles, and send out light and truth from its dark recesses. After weary months the king granted his release.

"Just at this time his father died, and left him all his estate. He was of a brave, generous nature, regretted his treatment of his only son, and died in peace with him. Penn made good use of his fortune. He fed many poor children whose parents were in the prisons and dungeons all over England for being true to their own consciences. He devoted all his time, talents, and influence to obtain from parliament some laws to protect the English people in the enjoyment of their religious liberty; but it was in vain. Despairing of any better fate for his poor persecuted brethren in the land of their birth, he cast his eyes over the waters and longed to build a quiet habitation for them in the wilderness. The good tidings of the prosperity and happiness of the Pilgrim settlements in their forest homes had traveled back to England, and Penn resolved now to lead his people thither. You know I told you that Penn's father had been a great favorite at court with the king and the royal family. He was one of the bravest officers in the British navy, and for his services to his country during the Dutch war he received a claim upon his government of sixteen thousand pounds. How much is that in our currency, Albert?"

"About eighty thousand dollars, aunty."

"Well, this King Charles was one of the greatest spendthrifts that ever lived, and of course was always in debt. Penn offered to take the amount of this claim in lands in America. He had much opposition from many lords and bishops, who could not endure to think of a Quaker colony being left in peace even three thousand miles away from them. Yet Penn had a great many influential friends at court, and finally the king, rather than pay the money, granted him a large tract of land on the western bank of the Delaware River, and named it Pennsylvania, or Penn's Woods. There were already some Dutch and Swedes living within the limits of this territory, and Penn immediately sent an agent over to tell them that he was coming out to live among them, to protect them and to do them good. He also wrote a letter to the sons of the forest, the Indians, telling them that they and he had the same Father, even the great God who made heaven and earth and all that it contains; that therefore they and he were brothers, and ought to love one another, and live in peace and good-will. His will was to be law throughout the colony, and he could have done much wrong to the people, and made himself rich by oppressing them, if he had been a selfish man; but fortunately he had but one wish, and that was that these people should be virtuous and happy. Then Penn made all his arrangements to lead out his colony to their new home. He left his beautiful and loving wife with his sweet children in England, that the children might be educated, admonishing her to 'live sparingly till my debts be paid;' for he had spent so much money helping the poor people that his own family were poor, and were obliged to live very frugally. All being ready, the Quaker colony embarked for America, and on the 27th of October, 1682, William Penn landed at New-castle, Delaware.

"The people crowded to the landing to wel-come the 'Quaker king,' for thus he was called, and indeed his power was absolute over the territory he now owned. He spoke kindly to them, exhorted them to industry and sobriety, and promised them his friendly offices to do them all the good in his power. With a few friends he left Newcastle in an open boat, and journeyed up the Delaware, in the soft, mellow November days, to the beautiful banks fringed with trees, on which the city of Philadelphia was soon to be laid out. Here he met the chiefs of the various Indian tribes. They as-sembled beneath a great elm-tree, and Penn told them that the English and the Indians were to obey the same laws, both were to be equally protected in their pursuits and posses-sions, and if any difficulty arose it should be settled by an equal number of English and Indians. 'We meet,' said he, 'on the broad pathway of good faith and good will. No ad-vantage shall be taken on either side, but all shall be openness and love. I will not call you children, for parents sometimes chide their children too severely. Nor brothers only; for brothers differ. The friendship between me and you I will not compare to a chain, for that the rains might rust or the falling tree might break. We are the same as if one man's body were to be divided into two parts; we are all one flesh and blood.' This treaty of peace and friendship was made under the open sky, by the side of the Delaware, with the sun and the river and the forest for witnesses. Penn came without arms ; he declared his purpose to abstain from violence. He had no message but peace ; and not a drop of Quaker blood was ever shed by an Indian. Here, on a neck of land between the Schuylkill and the Delaware, William Penn laid, at Philadelphia, the city of refuge, the mansion of freedom, the home of humanity. In after years 'Pennsylvania bound the northern and southern colonies in bonds stronger than chains ; Philadelphia was the birthplace of American Independence, and the pledge of Union.'

" For several years Penn remained with his colony, directing and ruling for its best interests, and his heart was gladdened with the sight of its prosperity and happiness. But he longed to sit once more at his own fireside, and look upon the dear home faces he had left. Besides, his colony was so well established, and governed by laws so mild and good, that the people had nothing to do but to be industrious, virtuous, and happy. Penn thought of the hundreds of English Quakers that still languished in dungeons and prisons. He felt that he must go back to England and do something for them. So he did ; he labored day and night, and was instrumental in obtaining the release of not less than twelve hundred Friends. But he pleaded not only for the Quakers, for his sympathies were large enough to take in all mankind ; and he, like Sir Harry Vane, claimed liberty of conscience for all men. He continued to watch over his American colony, sending out emigrants, and advancing its interests in every way. In extreme old age he writes to them as a father to his children, ' If the people want of me any thing that would make them happier, I should readily grant it.' He left the people of Pennsylvania free to alter their laws as they should think best, but the form of government devised by Penn's love and wisdom was so nearly perfect, that to this day its fundamental principles remain. These are some of the words of his farewell to his people : ' My love and my life are to you and with you, and no water can quench it nor distance bring it to an end. I have been with you, cared over you, and served you with unfeigned love ; and you are beloved of me and dear to me beyond utterance. You are come to a quiet land ; liberty and authority are in your hands. Rule for Him under whom the princes of this world will one day esteem it an honor to govern in their places. And thou, Philadelphia, the virgin settlement of this province, my soul prays to God for thee, that thou mayest stand in the day of trial, and that thy children may be blessed. Dear friends, my love salutes you all.'

" Now, Nannie, are you satisfied with your Quaker hero ? " said Aunt Edith, turning to the little girl beside her. But as Aunt Edith glanced from one to another of the little group of attentive listeners, she saw by the light that beamed from their bright eyes that it was unnecessary to take a vote on this subject.

CHAPTER VI.

The Carolinas and Georgia—Judith Menigault.

"TO-NIGHT, children, we must turn our thoughts southward, where the orange and the olive grow; where the scent of wild roses and magnolias perfume the air all the days of the livelong year; to the beautiful Carolinas, where Gilbert and Raleigh planted the first English colonies; and where, a hundred years before, the proud Spaniard roamed, seeking for Indian empire, and treasures of gold and silver. Do you remember his name, Harry?"

"O yes, aunty; how could I forget De Soto and his gay Spaniards, in their silks and glittering armor?"

"And their terrible disappointment," continued Nannie.

"And his death, and burial in the Mississippi," added Albert.

"What do you remember, Stevey?" asked Aunt Edith.

"Why, they were cruel, and chased the poor Indians with dogs, and cut off their fingers and hands, and put chains on them, and made slaves of them."

" Yes, so they did, Stevey ; they were a dark, ignorant race, not well instructed. It was a merciful Providence that did not allow them to settle and own these beautiful lands, which God kept for a different race, as I will show you. But, first, I want to tell you something about King Charles the Second, who was now on the throne of England. Those who have studied his history describe him as the weakest of men, though not naturally cruel. He was exceedingly ignorant ; I doubt if he could read as well as you can; Stevey. When he met his ministers in council over the most important matters, he brought his dog along to amuse him. He took little interest in any thing that was said, and if he spoke his speech was ' silly, idle, and frothy.' He wasted his time with the ladies and actresses of his' court, listening to their senseless talk and love songs. One of the most celebrated actresses of the court, and a great favorite with the king, was named Nelly Gwynn. She amused the king very much by taking off the Quakers. When drunk, which he was more or less every day, he was jolly and good-natured; and very generous. He would give away his own property or his neighbors' in kingly style.

"The courtiers and nobles did pretty much as they pleased with him, and each one looked after his own interest. A ridiculous picture of the king was made, in which he was represented with a woman on each arm, and his courtiers following and slyly picking his pocket. At one time, in a drunken fit of generosity, he gave away the whole of Virginia to one of his favorites, without regard to the charter granted by his grandfather to John Smith's company. That is to say, he might have Virginia if he could get it. Seeing that the king was generous, some of the nobility cast their longing eyes over upon the beautiful Carolina lands, and greatly desired to own them. The vine, the olive, the mulberry, and the silk-worm would flourish in that latitude, and would bring them golden harvests. There were eight of these covetous noblemen, and taking the king one day in pleasant mood he granted to them a charter for all the territory extending seven degrees north and south, and forty degrees east and west. That is, from the Atlantic to the Pacific Ocean, comprising what is now North and South Carolina, Georgia, Alabama, Mississippi, Louisiana, Arkansas, Tennessee, Missouri, and Texas, and also part of Mexico and Florida, which the Spaniards were under the impression belonged to them by the right of discovery and settlement."

"Well done!" exclaimed Albert; "that was a fine plantation; he must have been joking, aunty."

"Life was all a joke to King Charles, but, be that as it may, this noble company of English gentlemen were much pleased with the gift, and made great preparations for settling and governing their magnificent realm across the ocean, and employed the wisest and greatest minds of England to draw up a constitution. 'Man proposes and God disposes,' as we have seen before in looking at the early history of our country. This glorious land was not intended to be owned and governed by 'nobles after the flesh,' but as a refuge and a consolation for the persecuted and oppressed out of all lands: those who loved the truth more than their own lives; nature's noblemen, the honest sons of toil, and the builders of their own fortunes. The constitution was very much admired in England; indeed, it was pronounced 'without compare' for deep wisdom, and was intended to last forever. It was on this wise: the eight noblemen were to be absolute sovereigns over the whole territory, and it was to descend to their heirs through all time. The land was to be divided into counties of vast extent. There was to be an earl and two barons to each county, who were to do the governing. The settlers, who rented, but did not own, the lands, were to be called 'leet men,' and they and their children were to be 'leet men' forever. Of course they wanted as many settlers as possible to come over, and rent and cultivate the land ; so the constitution promised not to interfere with any on account of religion. But there was some little difficulty in getting this constitution to fit the new order of things in the wild woods of the Carolinas. Already there was a settlement of New England Puritans on the coast of North Carolina. They had been attracted thither by the beauty of the climate, and had purchased a title to their lands from the native Indians, and paid for them honestly. Many had also come into Carolina from the Virginia settlements. They were living here and there in little groups of humble but comfortable cabins, cultivating the soil, and enjoying life in great peace and comfort. Though they were an honest, simple people, yet they were brave and high spirited ; though they did not wish to be nobles and titled gentry, neither did they wish to descend to be 'leet men' forever."

"Just imagine," said Albert, "Earl Tobaccoplanter, Baron Cowherd, Lady Dairymaid, and Count Fisherman."

"Exactly so. For their government they had a few simple laws, which were administered by a council, who were elected by the people themselves, and these were found quite sufficient for their wants. So when the agent of the eight sovereigns arrived in the colony, and called the people together to explain the new state of things, and this great and beneficent constitution that had been prepared for them, these honest people looked one at another, and said to the agent in effect, 'Take it away; we don't want it; it doesn't suit us.' They continued to resist all attempts at interference with their simple forms of self-government, and the whole scheme fell through because it was against nature and human rights, both of which flourished and had full liberty to grow in this new country. So the people continued in quietness and peace to build houses, plant tobacco, raise corn and cattle, and catch fish. They were also careful that none should be persecuted for their religious opinions.

"The settlements pushed further and further south into South Carolina and Georgia, for it was a land of promise. A colony of Irish and Scotch Presbyterians, and a large company of

Huguenots, made their homes here. These were French Protestants who had suffered the most miserable cruelties from the Catholics. Thousands of them were put to death by the sword. Thousands more emigrated to Holland and England. They were a sober, industrious class of people, skillful in fine manufactures of various kinds, and at last the stupid and wicked French government began to understand that they were doing a very unwise thing to drive out of the country so industrious and thriving a people, who were gladly welcomed in other countries because of the skill and knowledge in their various trades which they introduced with them. The French authorities therefore made laws against emigration; they forbade their people to fly, and yet continued to persecute them with the greatest fury. They tortured them in different ways. Their ministers were broken on the wheel; their little children were torn from them in order that they might be educated to be Catholics. O the sufferings, the tears and groans of these poor people! Is it wonderful that they, too, longed for a quiet habitation in the wilderness, and that, notwithstanding the law against emigration, they stole out of the country by thousands, taking their little children with them? Some came to the New

England colonies, where they arrived destitute
of every thing.   But our Puritan fathers gave
them a warm welcome.   Collections were made
in the different towns to supply their wants,
and lands were given them.   Some took refuge
with the Quakers, and they were received as
brothers in adversity.   But the warm climate
of the Carolinas attracted the largest number,
for, you know, they came from the warm, sunny
climate of France.   Listen to the story of a
noble Huguenot woman.   'We quitted our home
by night, leaving all our worldly goods,' said
Judith, the young wife of Pierre Manigault.
'We hid ourselves for ten days while search
was made for us.   We stole round through
Germany and Holland over to England in the
depths of winter.   Having embarked at London,
the spotted fever appeared on board the vessel.
Many died, among them our aged mother.   We
touched at Bermuda, where our vessel was
seized.   Our money was all spent ; with difficulty we procured a passage on another vessel.
After our arrival in Carolina we suffered every
kind of evil.   Our eldest brother died of hard
labor, to which he was unaccustomed.   Since
leaving France we have experienced every kind
of affliction—disease, pestilence, famine, poverty, and hard labor.   I have worked the ground

a slave, and often had not bread when I wanted it. Yet,' adds this excellent woman, in a spirit of grateful resignation, 'God has done great things for us in enabling us to bear up under so many trials.' You may take her for your heroine this evening, children. 'Judith Manigault, the Huguenot refugee.'

"Thus the Huguenots settled on the lands near Charleston, and on the banks of the Santee River. Here they built their neat cottages and found rest. The melody of their psalms and hymns filled the scented groves, and rose as sweet incense to the King of kings. Thus were the Carolinas settled, and that territory which was afterward separated and called Georgia. In both Carolinas, in the year 1688, the population amounted to about eight thousand."

CHAPTER VII.

Enemies Across the Sea—First Dream of "Union."

" LET us pause long enough, children, to take a backward glance over the path we have traveled. Let us keep our facts well strung together, as you do your beads, Nannie. What date did I give you last night for the settlement of the Carolinas?"

Nannie replied, " 1688."

" How long was that after the discovery by Columbus, Albert?"

" One hundred and ninety-six years, aunty."

" Yes, nearly two centuries. In the first hundred years what was accomplished?"

" The country was examined and explored by the Spanish, French, and English," continued Albert, " and description and accurate maps made of it."

" Very well answered. It was proved beyond a doubt to be the 'goodliest land' the sun shone on for the richness of its soil, its noble rivers, safe and commodious harbors, and beautiful climate. And what was done during the next century, Harry?"

"It was settled along the eastern coast, principally by the English."

"Nannie, give me the name and date of the settlements in their order."

"Shall I mention Sir Walter Raleigh's colony in North Carolina in 1590?"

"No; that perished. You may commence with the first successful settlement."

"Well, aunty, that was at Jamestown, in Virginia, in 1606, by John Smith's company."

"Yes, they were sent out at the expense of a company of London merchants, who expected and realized large revenues from trading with the colonists."

"The second settlement was Maryland."

"No," interrupted Harry; "the Pilgrim Fathers came next."

"O yes, so they did, in 1620, and settled on the eastern coast of Massachusetts."

"Quite right; they came at their own expense, that is, they borrowed the money from some London merchants, and paid it afterward from the fruits of their labors. They fled from persecution to a land where they might worship God according to their own consciences. The next colony, Nannie?"

"Was Maryland, settled by the Catholics under the good Sir George Calvert."

" Yes, this was the only Catholic colony, and they came also to escape persecution. Next ? "

Nannie looked puzzled and Albert came to her assistance :

" The Dutch colonies came next in order."

" Yes, the Dutch in New York, and the Swedes in New Jersey and Delaware. These colonies were planted between 1630 and 1650. What became of them, Albert ? "

" During the war between the Dutch and English, England sent a fleet here, took possession of the Dutch colonies, and added them to hers."

" What became of the Swedish colonies ? "

" After the death of the good king Gustavus Adolphus they languished, and gradually mingled with the English colonies around them."

" Correctly answered. I am pleased you remember so well, Albert. Which colony dates next, Nannie ? "

" The Quaker settlement, on the Delaware, by the good William Penn, in 1682."

" Which next, Harry ? "

" The Carolinas."

" Yes, and Georgia, between the years 1660 and 1685 ; settled by Protestant refugees from Ireland, Scotland, and England, and by French Huguenots. Well now, we have the whole east-

7

ern coast of North America settled from Maine to Georgia, comprising the original thirteen English colonies. The whole population amounted to about two hundred thousand, of which number nearly one half peopled the New England colonies. Observe, children, how all the European nations contributed to lay the foundations of this great American nation. Italy gave the discoverers—Columbus and the Cabots—though it was the enterprise and liberality of a Spanish queen that furnished the first vessels which reached these shores. Then Spanish, French, and English explorers and adventurers eagerly searched out the land and brought back their goodly reports of it. It was meet and right that it should be the refuge of humanity. England, Ireland, Scotland, Sweden, Germany, and France furnished its early settlers. There should be no American nationality save what is to be found in the principles of our civil and religious liberty—that Christian idea of liberty, equality, and brotherhood which we learn from the Gospel of our Lord and Saviour Jesus Christ. Our fathers were Protestants except in Maryland ; but even here, all sects being tolerated, the Protestants emigrated faster than the Catholics and soon outnumbered them. They were the children of sorrow, suffering, and poverty ; they had escaped to a goodly land, a land of plenty, where there was enough for every man who was willing to toil, without wronging his brother. All things considered, they were the happiest and most virtuous people the sun shone upon. Hear the testimony of an English traveler of high rank, who made the tour of the colonies to observe their manners and customs : 'I have observed here,' said he, 'less swearing and profaneness, less drunkenness and debauchery, less uncharitable feuds and animosities, and less knaveries and villanies, than in any part of the world where my lot has been.' Yet they were not without their troubles. The colonies had frequent disputes about their boundaries, and between Virginia and Maryland it went so far as the shedding of blood. Then, too, the Indians, who had been friendly to the early settlers, began now to be alarmed at the vast numbers of whites that were flocking to the country, and they feared they would be driven entirely from their homes and lands. The Dutch had taught them to drink whisky. They had been sometimes cruelly treated by bad men, for there are bad men in every community. Now, revenge is the highest virtue the Indian knows, and when they turned upon their enemies they remembered no mercy in their wrath. The Dutch were often at war with the Indians. This involved the New England colonies also, and they suffered severely in this respect.

"Still another trouble was, that the colonists were conscious they had many enemies at home, who viewed their growth and prosperity with an envious eye. These enemies hated the doctrines and opinions of those who had escaped from their persecutions beyond the seas, and refused to have kings or nobles to rule over them, and believed in the right and capacity of men to govern themselves. This party in England said continually among themselves, these 'rogues and rascals'—for so they were pleased to call them—'will increase in numbers, wealth, and power, and after awhile they will break away entirely from their allegiance to England and declare their independence.' They talked thus to King Charles and advised him to take away their charters. But King Charles loved his own ease, and continued to amuse himself with his dogs and his actresses, and it really was a good thing for the colonies that so weak and indolent a king sat on the throne of England, for it gave them opportunity to grow and become strong and rich, so that when the time came to resist English tyranny they were able to do it. But

at last King Charles died, and died as he had
lived. The cares of his kingdom never seemed
to enter his mind, and his last words were
a charge that they should take good care of
Nelly Gwynn. His brother James ascended
the throne, because Charles had no son to take
his place. James pretended to be a Protestant,
because otherwise he could not have been king,
but really at heart he was a Catholic. He
looked with an evil eye at these American colonies, for he considered them a hot-bed of Protestantism and rebellion against royalty. King
James was right. The Catholic Church and
the Church of England were arrayed on the
side of kings and a privileged few ; but American Protestantism is favorable to the people of
all classes, conditions, and races King James
determined to oppress them ; so he sent over
one Andross to unite all the New England
colonies into one, and he was to rule as royal
governor, appointed by the king. The New
England colonies were more disliked in England
than the others ; they were more feared for
their large population as well as for their wealth
and intelligence. There was a mighty throb-
bing of the New England heart when this news
was received. A day of fasting and prayer
was appointed, and their ministers exhorted the

people from their pulpits to stand up in defense of their political rights, and not yield the liberties that had been purchased by so much toil and suffering. They sent respectful petitions to the king not to interfere with them in their civil and religious rights. They reminded him that they had made their own homes in the wilderness without any expense to the government of England; that it was a natural right for any man to expatriate himself—that is, to go out from the land of his birth—and if he left her protection he no longer owed obedience to her laws. They appealed to the king's better feelings in these words: 'We could not live without the public worship of God. That we might enjoy this without human mixtures, we, not without tears, departed from our country, kindred, and fathers' houses. Our garments are become old by reason of the long journey; ourselves, who came away in our strength, are, many of us, become old and gray-headed, and some of us stooping for age. God knows our greatest ambition is to live a quiet life in a corner of the world.'

"All this talk of natural right and justice was an unknown tongue to King James; the idea was too large to get into his small brain; and in due time the royal governor made his appear-

ance in scarlet and lace. He began to tax and
plunder the people, and fill his own pockets
without scruple. Moreover he ordered the service of the English Church to be read in the
churches of Boston. This stirred the hearts of
the old Puritans to the deepest depth. They
pleaded their chartered privileges against his
taxes. He told them the king had recalled
their charters. 'Do you think,' said he, 'that
Tom and Joe may tell the king what money he
may have.' They produced their titles to their
lands that they had purchased from the Indians,
the original owners of the soil. Andross replied
that it was 'worth no more than the scratch of
a bear's paw.' But an honest Puritan minister,
John Higginson, told Andross that they went
back from all charters and human laws to the
book of Genesis, where 'God gave the earth to
the sons of Adam to be subdued and replen-
ished,' and declared that 'the people of New
England held their lands from the grand charter
of the King of kings.'"

"That was a good point, aunty," said Albert.
"What did Andross say to that?"

"Why, he called him a 'rebel,' and threatened to deal with him. Bloodshed would have
followed, for these New England fathers loved
their liberties more ᵗhan their lives, but fortu-

nately King James had become very unpopular in England. His own children conspired against him. He was accused of being a Catholic in disguise, and was driven from the throne into exile. His daughter Mary, and her husband, William of Orange, ascended the throne. They were Protestants, and were more friendly to the American colonies. When this good news came, Andross was ordered by the authorities to quit the country forthwith. Indeed, he made all haste to do so, and thought himself happy to escape in safety from the people he had insulted and outraged. The good people of New England, and, indeed, of all the colonies, felt a sense of relief when they knew that he was fairly out of the country, for they were aware that the fate of the New England colonies would be sure to be theirs in due order, for their interests were one. In this attempt at tyranny King James had, without intending it, done a good work for America. He had consolidated New England, that is, united them in order that Andross might more conveniently tax and oppress them. In the presence of this danger to their liberties, the hearts of the people flowed together as they never had before, and they had joined hand in hand to resist the oppression. They thus early learned that in their union was their strength. This idea grew and strengthened from this time, and the people of the different colonies saw more and more that their interests were one. Thus good came out of apparent evil. That glorious idea of union took deep root in the American heart, and afterward resulted in that more perfect union that is to-day the corner-stone of our national greatness."

CHAPTER VIII.

French War—French Jealousy and French Intrigues.

"WHERE did we break off last evening, children?" inquired Aunt Edith.

"They had just driven Andross out of New England, who had taxed and plundered them and taken away their liberties by order of King James," answered Albert.

"Very true. Why did I say that this attempt at tyranny was an advantage to the country?"

"Because," added Nannie, "it put the idea of 'union' into the minds of the colonists."

"Right, Nannie. Now keep the thread of the story. Andross was driven home about the year 1690. What befell King James?"

"The English people hated him, and drove him from the throne, and he fled from the kingdom."

"True, and they then invited William, Prince of Orange, a Hollander, who had married Mary, the daughter of King James, to come over and rule them. By doing this the English people established the principle that the British Constitution governs the king as well as the subject,

and is the supreme authority in the land. After
the death of William and Mary, and of Queen
Anne, their successor, the House of Hanover
ruled England, in the persons of the Kings
George First, Second, and Third. They were
more German than English, and were more interested in European than American affairs.
This was a great blessing to America, for all
she needed was just to be 'let alone.' This
English neglect was very wholesome. For the
next fifty years the colonies grew stronger and
richer. They planted and reaped, and their
store-houses were full. They increased rapidly
in population, they pushed further and further
into the wilderness, turning its wild wastes into
smiling fields of plenty. In New York the
English settlements were pushing westward to
the lakes, and in Pennsylvania and Virginia
westward to the Ohio River. So far as concerned the colonies themselves, peace, prosperity, and happiness nestled in her beautiful
valleys and crowned her glorious hill-tops. How
different from the scenes that had been and
still were enacting on the other side of the Atlantic! With only short intervals of rest, Europe had been for nearly two centuries cursed
with war. With whatever political strifes em-
broiled the nations there inevitably mingled

that old undercurrent of religious difference. It was the irrepressible conflict of Protestantism and Catholicism, England leading the Protestant nations and France the Catholic, while Germany was the battle-ground. A fierce, cruel wrestle they had of it through the long and weary years, and unfortunately their quarrels were not confined to European soil, but extended to their possessions and colonies all over the world. Again and again the strifes of the Old World stained the soil of the New with blood. In the space of seventy-one years, from 1689 to 1760, the American colonies were involved in four wars, occupying in all twenty-seven years. This included the French and Indian war of which I am now about to tell you. The French, you know, had settled Canada, which lay north of our New England colonies. It was a French Catholic province. They had also settled around the great lakes, and laid claim to the West, the valley of the Mississippi, down to Louisiana. They were jealous of the English because of their rich American colonies. They resolved that England should not own the whole of this vast continent, so they built a chain of forts from Canada to the Ohio River, and declared that England should not pass the river nor occupy the lands west of it.

Of course our fathers took sides with England, for they had no sympathy with French Catholics and did not want them for neighbors. They preferred that the whole continent should be Protestant if possible, so they left the plow, and buckled on the sword and shouldered the musket. Those who remained at home when they assembled for public worship, or when they knelt at their home altars, sent up fervent prayers that God would give the victory to the right. The French induced the Canadian Indians to join with them against the English and against our fathers. They had a fearful struggle, and English and American blood flowed like water before the strife ended. But the God of battles gave the victory to the cause of Protestantism both in America and in Europe. The Catholic nations were baffled and driven back in confusion, and England came out of the contest greater and stronger than ever. When at last a treaty of peace was signed in Paris in 1763, her American colonial possessions stretched from the Mississippi to the Atlantic Ocean, and from the Gulf of Mexico to Hudson's Bay; for Canada was now an English province. Our fathers gave thanks for the victory, gladly laid aside their swords, and resumed their peaceful pursuits.

"Not only in America and Europe did England triumph over France, but He in whose hands 'are the corners of the earth' gave her the victory wherever the conflict raged. France came out of the struggle defeated and despoiled of her possessions. She lost her settlements in Africa, while in India and the adjacent islands her power was shattered, and the Empire of the East was given to England, who holds it to this day.

"I have now described the French war, as it is called in American history. You have seen that to the French it resulted in the loss of Canada, as well as all the territory of the West. But though England was now at the very height of power, she had many enemies. All the Catholic nations of Europe hated her, and the Protestant nations envied and feared her. The English were a great nation, certainly, but haughty and domineering; always looking to their own interests at their neighbor's expense, and seeking the lion's share in every bargain. England owned rich colonies and islands in the East and West Indies; but the source of her greatest revenues were her American colonies. Give me your attention, children, and I will explain how this was.

"England is a great manufacturing country.

The Americans at that time were principally farmers and planters, or fishermen. The English parliament had from the first settlement of the colonies made all laws concerning commerce and trade between America and England. By these laws the colonists were obliged to take all the productions of this country, over and above what they used, into English markets, and to no other. Tobacco, grain, wool, iron, and other articles, all went to England to be manufactured. Other laws compelled the Americans to buy all they wanted from the shops of England. Now this was a great advantage to England, but not to America. You know, boys, if you have any thing to sell, you would like to sell it to the boy who would pay you most for it; and, Nannie, if you and I go shopping we shouldn't want to buy at one particular shop whether we liked the article or not, or whether we paid more for it than we could buy it for elsewhere. America was the largest customer England had. The population had increased so rapidly that they purchased millions of dollars' worth of British goods every year. But though the advantage was all on the side of England, the Americans submitted cheerfully in consideration of the advantages they derived in many ways from the British merchants, who had been always liberal to them. You remember it was a company of London merchants who sent out John Smith's colony, and they also lent our Pilgrim Fathers money to bring them here. They afterward generously advanced them money on many occasions to make such improvements as building bridges, making roads, and draining marshes.

" The possession of these colonies by England made her an object of jealousy to all Europe, but especially to France, whose national pride was stung to the quick by her losses during the late war, especially the loss of Canada. Her only hope of crippling the power of England was to separate the hearts of her colonists from her, and induce them to declare themselves independent. They lost no opportunity of making mischief between the two countries, and the French Government went so far as to send secret emissaries to America to travel through the country to sow the seeds of discord. They tried to arouse the pride and ambition of the Americans by descanting upon their wealth, power, and rapidly-increasing population ; telling them they were no longer in their infancy, but were strong enough to declare themselves a nation, free and independent. They talked much of England's tyranny, her oppressive laws

and acts of parliament, that crippled American
commerce and manufactures only to fill the
pockets of English merchants and mechanics.
With many other arguments of this sort, they
predicted still more oppressive laws and further
acts of tyranny, and counseled the Americans
to be ready for resistance. They found many
who lent an eager ear to these suggestions ;
but there is no doubt a very large majority of
the American people were satisfied with their
connection with England, and were happy in
being called British subjects, so that if the
mother country had treated her American colonies kindly these foreign mischief-makers would
have failed utterly to accomplish their designs.
But she did not.

"England was intoxicated with her glory and
her power. All Europe trembled before her,
and she was mistress of the ocean. King
George III. and his ministers thought that the
long-wished-for opportunity was now come to
make the kingly authority felt and acknowledged
in America. You remember I told you that
our fathers had enemies in England who dis-
trusted them, and often predicted that one day
they would rebel and escape from British rule.
These enemies were principally among the
nobles, the dignitaries of the English Church,

8

and the king's ministers. King George was a devotee to the doctrine of the divine right of kings, and thought the American people had too much political liberty. The true friends of America were mainly among the middle classes, the British merchants and Dissenters. Moreover, though England had emerged from her long wars splendid in her outward pomp and glory, yet we must remember that war is very expensive, and that nations pay dearly for its glories and its triumphs. England was burdened with an immense debt, and her people groaned under heavy taxes. 'Now,' thought the English ministers and the parliament, 'now is the time to make proof of our power over the Americans by laying taxes upon them, and thus relieve the English people from such a weight as oppresses them.' But the Americans declared that they would not be taxed by an English parliament, three thousand miles away, whose members never saw America. The English parliament consists of two bodies called the House of Lords and the House of Commons. They do not in all respects correspond to our Senate and House of Representatives, though they make laws for the English people, just as our representatives do for us.

"America had no representatives in parliament, no voice in any of its acts, and they re-solved there should be 'no taxation without representation.' That became the watchword of the country. The English in turn contended that America ought to be willing to be taxed and help to pay the expenses of the late war, since it had cost England a great deal to send her ships of war and armies to America to beat back the French and Indians and secure peace. The Americans admitted that they owed a debt both of gratitude and money to the mother country, and they were quite willing to pay it, but they must be allowed to lay the taxes upon themselves. Each colony was governed by an assembly composed of representatives elected by their own people, who made all laws, and laid all taxes, just as parliament did for England. Each colony would be willing to pay her pro-portion of whatever England thought was justly due her.

"They sent agents over to the king and par-liament to make known their determination in respectful language. And they also desired that England would recall the British soldiers from America, since they were now at peace, and it was a useless expense to maintain them here."

"I don't see," said Nannie, "how the fathers

could have been more reasonable or more in the right."

"Well, it looked so from this side of the ocean, but to-morrow evening I'll tell you how it looked from the other side."

CHAPTER IX.

British Stupidity—Taxation and Tyranny—William Pitt—"Sons of Liberty"—South Carolina and Massachusetts say, "We be Brethren."

"I AM to tell you this evening, children, that the British ministers and King George were very angry at what they called the obstinacy and ingratitude of the Americans in refusing to submit to be taxed, and they resolved that they would compel them to submission. They therefore refused to recall their army home, under pretense that it was necessary to overawe the Indians and keep the peace. But New England was as keen-sighted as Old England. The Americans saw quite through this false excuse, and felt sure that the army was kept here to overawe them. The parliament proceeded soon after to pass several very irritating and tyrannical acts. One of these forbade the colonies to trade with each other. Another forbade mechanics to have more than two apprentices. Still another declared that lumber, pitch, and pine-trees should be cut only within certain limits. Another interrupted the commerce that had always been carried on between the colonies and the West Indies, which was a great source of wealth to the Americans, and also a great convenience, as they obtained from the Islands silver and gold with which they paid their debts to British merchants. This unwise and provoking legislation of parliament only roused the indignation of the people, and drove them to unite in their opposition to such a system of tyranny. They petitioned and protested, but the ministers and the king and parliament blindly persisted in their mad resolution to conquer and break the proud spirit of the Americans. They followed up these acts by another called the Stamp Act, the most unpopular measure ever tried with the colonists. This news was received in America with a perfect storm of indignation, that swept over the land from Maine to Georgia. The hearts of the people throbbed together as one heart. They organized themselves under the name of 'Sons of Liberty' in all the colonies, and pledged themselves to stand by each other. I see you are curious to know what the Stamp Act was. It was a law which required all bonds, notes, and such like papers used by the colonists to have stamps on them, the stamps being a tax so much over and above the real value of the papers. No other paper was legal. It was a very skillfully-devised measure, and, if it could have been enforced, would have brought in a large revenue, for nearly every body must use such paper. .

"The people were infuriated. In New England they mobbed·the houses of the men who had been appointed stamp-officers, and compelled them to fly for their lives. They also entered into a solemn league to neither buy nor use British goods until this Stamp Act was repealed. They likewise called a congress of delegates from the various colonies to meet in New York in October, 1765. They met and drew up their petitions to the king, the House of Lords, and House of Commons. The British merchants, alarmed at the resolutions of the Americans to buy no more of their wares, presented their petitions to parliament, picturing to them the ruin that would follow to England if the Americans were driven to extremities by these unjust measures, and praying parliament to repeal this obnoxious act and restore good feeling between the two countries. The ministers were now alarmed. Of all things they dreaded an American congress, and they called before them Benjamin Franklin, one of the American agents, to question him on these subjects.

"This man began life as an apprentice to a printer in Boston, and he struggled up to occupy one of the proudest positions ever reached by man. His fame had gone before him, and now he verified the truth of the inspired proverb, 'Seest thou a man diligent in his business? he shall stand before kings.' When it was known that Benjamin Franklin would speak in the House of Lords, the galleries were crowded to hear him. He reasoned the subject with great dignity, calmness, and presence of mind, and produced a profound impression. William Pitt, the greatest of English statesmen, also took his stand on the side of the colonies, in a speech of great power and eloquence, and obtained the repeal of the Stamp Act. This happy news was received, both in England and America, with universal rejoicings, ringing of bells, bonfires, and devout thanksgiving. These demonstrations were sincere in both countries, for the loss by the interruptions of commerce had been great, and the prospect of civil war terrible to contemplate. The Assembly of Massachusetts voted thanks to the great statesman, William Pitt, who had pleaded for the colonies, and the Assembly of Virginia ordered a statue to the king and the illustrious men who had acknowledged the justice of their cause. Yet, after

all, it was more a hope than a faith that the
Americans cherished in the good intentions of
England toward them. Though they were un-
willing to confess it, confidence was gone."

"O what a pity!" said little Stevey, mournfully.

"It seemed so indeed, my little boy, though
evil often changes to good, and sorrow into joy.
You must remember, children, that the first
generation of settlers before whose stalwart
arms the forests had bowed, whose hands planted the first fields and reared the first cabins in
the wilderness, had passed away. England was
the land of their birth, the home of their youth.
But they were gone. Their children, born and
reared here, knew no country, loved no country,
in comparison with America. They knew nothing of kingly splendor, court pageantry, and
privileged orders. Time had weakened the ties
between the mother country and her colonies.
The calm that succeeded for the next few years
was not without omens of that fierce storm
which was soon to sweep and desolate the land
with the fire and sword of civil war."

"What does civil war mean, aunty?" asked
Harry.

"War between people of the same nation.
The Americans were English subjects as much
as those who lived in England. There were

also even in America quite a number who were willing to submit to the king, and who refused to take any part in the rebellion, while a good many actually joined the king's armies, and fought against their countrymen and friends. They hated each other bitterly. Even families were divided ; father against son, and brother against brother. Civil war is the saddest, most sorrowful, and cruel of all war. But I was about to tell you of King George. He was always sorry that he had allowed the repeal of the Stamp Act, and he was still determined to punish and conquer the Americans. Indeed, he thought it his first duty to maintain the dignity of kingly authority.

"William Pitt, also called Earl of Chatham, the great statesman who had ruled in the councils of England for so many years, whose genius and wisdom had brought her· to such a height of power and splendor, was too old and feeble longer to hold the helm of state. He and his associates were succeeded by other and inferior men, who were more willing to follow the councils and wishes of the stubborn and blind king. They soon brought into parliament a bill to impose taxes on tea, glass, and paints. It was immediately passed and approved by the king. The revenues from the taxes were to be applied to pay the salaries of the governors and judges of the colonies. This was worse than ever, for the colonies had always paid their own officers from their own treasuries ; but now they would be entirely in the interest of the king who paid them. They said at once, 'We wont submit to it.' New England, New York, Virginia, Maryland, and South Carolina spoke it out very loud and distinctly. Committees of correspondence between the 'Sons of Liberty' were organized in every colony, and a constant interchange of views and purposes was kept up. They entered into a League and Covenant not to import nor use British goods or manufactures, and they faithfully adhered to it. They were to act in concert and keep faith with one another, and stand or fall together. The English were frightened again, and repealed all except the tax on tea. The Americans were firm. Not a pound of it should land. It was the principle, not the tax, that they contended against. When the tea reached New York and Philadelphia no one had the courage to receive it, lest their houses should be pulled down about their heads. In Charleston some was taken ashore and secreted in damp cellars, where it soon spoiled. At Boston notice was several times given to the ships to sail out of the harbor and return the tea to its owners. As this order was not complied with, twenty men, disguised as Indians, went quietly aboard under cover of night, and in a few moments three hundred and forty chests of tea were emptied into Boston harbor. And this is the famous 'Boston Tea Party' you have so often heard of. A large crowd of the friends of these men stood on shore until the deed was accomplished, and then all retired quietly to their homes.

"When tidings of these things reached England the ministers and the king, and all who were of their opinions, were enraged out of measure at the obstinate resistance of these American 'rogues and rascals' to the English crown and parliament. Orders were sent out to General Gage, a British officer who was at New York, to proceed immediately to Boston with two regiments of soldiers. His squadron of fourteen ships also took position to command the city. He landed his troops and ordered them to invest the city, and they occupied the State House by direction of the royal governor, Sir Francis Bernard. The Americans were indignant to see their State-House, sacred in their eyes, defiled by the presence of an armed foe. Guards challenged them at the street corners as they went about their daily vocations;

constant sources of irritation arose and embittered the citizens and soldiery, until at length
it ended in a street-fight between the soldiers
and an armed band of citizens, in which three
were killed and several wounded. The citizens
gathered by thousands, and the governor thought
it prudent to remove the soldiers. All these
events had no other effect upon the king, his
ministers, and parliament than to harden their
hearts like Pharaoh of old. His prime minister,
Lord North, at once introduced a bill, called the
'Port Bill,' cutting off all commerce and trade
with Boston from any quarter. It was to go
into effect June 1, 1774, after which no ship
was to load or unload within her harbor, and
the offices of custom were to be removed to the
neighboring town of Salem. Lord North said
this was because 'from this city of Boston has
issued all the mischief which disturbs the colonies, and all the venom which infests America.'
Now this was a heavy blow, for the wealth of
Boston was her commerce, and she was the
largest and richest of American cities. The
execution of this port bill would bring her to
ruin, and they had no power to resist, because
General Gage was now military governor of
the province; his soldiers held the city, and his
ships of war her harbor.

ow' The English government thought by these
severe means at once to punish and make an
example of Boston, and intimidate the other
colonies from imitating her. But they failed
utterly to accomplish their object. From far
and near came words of sympathy and cheer.
The first of June was observed as a day of
mourning throughout the land. In all the cities
the stores were closed, and the bells tolled for
the misfortunes of their brethren of Boston.
They declared that their interests and their
destinies should be one with hers, and the inhabitants of Salem and the other ports, whom
the English government supposed would selfishly rejoice in the removal of commerce to
their towns, generously offered the Bostonians
their wharves and warehouses free of expense.
Great distress and suffering prevailed in Boston.
Their rich men were now poor, and their laboring classes on the point of starvation. But
from every colony came not only the blessing
of good words, but gifts of substantial relief.
The warm heart of South Carolina, child of the
sun, throbbed right against the heart of Massachusetts. Her people were the first to minister
to the sufferers, sending early in June two hundred barrels of rice, with word that six hundred
more would follow. At Wilmington, North

Carolina, two hundred pounds currency were raised in a few days. Lord North had laughed at the idea of American union, calling it 'a rope of sand.' 'It is a rope,' said the people of Wilmington, 'that will hang him.' The New England colonies made offerings of sheep, cattle, fish, and flour; in short, 'whatever the land or the hook and line could furnish.' Even the French in Canada sent over a thousand bushels of wheat. Delaware, Maryland, and Virginia contributed. In Fairfax County, where Washington presided at a meeting, he headed the subscription paper with a gift of fifty pounds. Away in the Valley of Virginia, beyond the Blue Ridge, the hardy mountaineers dedicated to Boston the first-fruits of their fields that the sun of 1774 should ripen. When the grain was golden they threshed and ground it, loaded their wagons and dragged it over the rude mountain-passes, and quietly delivered at Frederick, Maryland, one hundred and thirty-seven barrels of flour as their gift to the sufferers of Boston, whose cause was also their cause.

"Cheered by such sympathy, Boston sent word back that they should endure to the end, 'trusting in God that these things would be overruled for the establishment of liberty, virtue, and happiness in America.'"

CHAPTER X.

King George Insults Benjamin Franklin—Lexington
and Concord Avenge the Insult—First Congress.

THE old year had gone out and the new
year had come in since Aunt Edith and
the children met for their evening history
lesson. Christmas and New Year, too, were
come and gone. The holidays had brought the
father home to his fireside, and well pleased was
he to find that his children had redeemed an
hour from each day's play to such good uses.
As he sat beside the evening firelight, Stevey
on one knee and Grace on the other, he listened
with relish to the children's glib descriptions
of the relative merits of Columbus and John
Smith, Raleigh and William Penn, occasionally
throwing in a fire of cross questions upon the
little group, and praising their ready replies.
As a reward for their attention he promised
to select for them a library of American biog-
raphy, that they might come to know still more
intimately the hero ancestry of their country.
Aunt Edith had spent her Christmas twenty
miles away, at the manor, with Uncle Jesse and

Aunt Rachel; but she was back now, to the children's delight, bringing with her Cousin Alice, a golden-haired little girl just Harry's age. All day Aunt Edith had been listening to the children's tales of Christmas, looking at their gifts—parlor-skates, sleds, crying-babies, marvelous games, and, best of all, a beautiful pony, that Stevey had named "Harry Vane." He was so gentle that Nannie had had more than one gallop over the hill, and twice he had drawn Stevey in his little cushioned wagon down to the pond to see the boys skate. When six o'clock came, however, they were ready for their history lesson, delighted to have another member for their class; for Cousin Alice was to stay some time, and Harry had tried to tell her all he remembered of the beautiful story of our country's childhood.

"Now, Harry," said Aunt Edith, "if you are not too tired of talking, I would like you to tell me the position of affairs, as well as you re-member it."

"Yes. I remember it well: General Gage with fourteen ships of war in Boston harbor, British soldiers holding the city, the people starving but for the charity of their neighbors, and not a sign of yielding."

"Very well, my boy. The Bostonians showed

9

themselves true sons of noble sires. Even the
laborers and carpenters, though often in extremity for food, refused to build barracks for
the British officers, or turn a spade on the fortifications with which their enemies were encir-
cling the city. Meantime, across the Atlantic,
there stood before the king and thirty-five Lords
of Council, pleading the cause of his country,
Benjamin Franklin, once the poor printer-ap-

FRANKLIN.

prentice-boy, but now the gray-haired philos-
opher whom all Europe honored. Against him
were arrayed nobles and ministry, parliament,

court, and king; but Franklin was the real king amid them all. Unable to set aside his facts or out-argue him, they tried to cover his good name with infamy, but he made a brave defense. The king, however, pretended to believe the false accusation of one of the ministers, named Wedderburn, and insulted Franklin as the plebeian representative of a nation of plebeians. Franklin shortly after embarked for his own land, 'to spread the celestial fire of freedom among men, and to make his name a cherished household word in every nation of Europe. When he died,' continues the historian, 'he had nations for his mourners, and the great and good throughout the world as his eulogists. When Wedderburn died no senate spoke his praise, no poet embalmed his memory; and even his king, hearing that he was dead, said only, " He has not left a greater knave behind him in my dominions." And who were' the thirty Lords of the Council that thought to mark and brand the noblest representative of free labor, who for many a year had earned his daily bread as apprentice, and knew the heart of the working man. If they had never come into being, whom among them would humanity have missed? But how would it have suffered if Franklin had not lived?'

"A few months after, the first American Congress convened at Philadelphia, the city built by William Penn, perhaps the purest among the immortal workmen who wrought and laid the foundations of the Republic; for which he had, in his old age, uttered this prayer: 'And thou, Philadelphia, my soul prays to God for thee, that thou mayest *stand in the day of trial.*' This congress was composed of delegates elected and sent by the people of each colony. Arriving in Philadelphia, the State-House was offered for their use, but the carpenters of the city also offered their plain but spacious hall, and the delicacy and courtesy of these American noblemen of the first congress was shown in their acceptance of the mechanics' offer. It was proposed that their deliberations should be prefaced and sanctified with prayer. Some members objected on account of the diversity of religious views of the body; but Samuel Adams, Puritan born, Puritan descended, said, 'I am no bigot. I can hear a prayer from any man of piety and virtue who is at the same time a friend to his country.' He then nominated Duché, an Episcopal clergyman, for the service. There stood reverently in prayer, Washington, Henry, Randolph, Lee, Jay, Rutledge, Gadsden, Livingston, Sherman, and the

Adamses. The psalm for the day was the voice of each heart: 'O Lord, fight thou against them that fight against me. Lord, who is like unto thee, who deliverest the poor from him that is too strong for him.' After the psalm the minister burst into an extempore prayer for America, Congress, Massachusetts, and especially for Boston. Peyton Randolph, of Virginia, was chosen president of the congress. Then a long, deep silence fell upon the assembly. The clock of time had never told a more important hour than this. The hopes of the human race rested heavily on their wisdom and courage. Deeply as they felt this, yet they little comprehended the light that should stream down the ages from the beacons their hands hung out from Independence Hall. 'They builded better than they knew.'

"They first decided the method of voting. Massachusetts and Virginia were by far the largest and most populous of the colonies ; it was argued by some that they should have a larger voice in the decisions of congress. But the delegate from New Hampshire said, 'A little colony has its *all* at stake as well as a great one.' They concluded that each colony should have one vote. Again they sat in silence. Who should speak, and utter the mind and heart of the assembly? Massachusetts had already spoken by the blood of her citizens slain in her streets by British soldiery, and by the patient endurance of the beleaguered city of Boston. The voice of Virginia was waited for. At last she spoke. Patrick Henry, the orator of the Revolution, arose and poured forth a tide of eloquence. He recited the wrongs of America, the tyranny of the king, and the unconstitutional acts of the British Parliament, and declared that 'all government was dissolved, and they were now reduced to a state of nature.' Then these brave words thrilled through the assembly: 'British oppression has effaced the boundaries of the several colonies; the distinctions between Virginians, Pennsylvanians, New Yorkers, and New Englanders are no more. *I am not a Virginian, but an American.'* ·

"Now you must understand, children, that our fathers, by calling a general American congress, laid themselves open to the charge of treason. They had no legal right to convene such an assembly; they set aside their charters, and their governors, and all authority, by so doing. Therefore they were very careful in their proceedings, and exceedingly moderate in their language. The great majority of the

people of all the colonies were still satisfied to
live and die subjects of King George the Third
and the British government ; indeed, they preferred it, if the rights of British subjects could
be secured to them. Thus they instructed the
men they sent to the first Congress. They were
to seek by every means to restore peace and
confidence between America and the mother
country ; armed resistance was deplored as the
last resort, to be tried only when every other
hope vanished. The Congress therefore decided once more to petition the king and the
parliament. They also issued an address to the
English people as fellow-countrymen, to the
Canadians also, and one to the American people,
setting forth the justice of their cause. They
then adjourned. The Canadians received the
address with some favor. Canada, you remember, had not been many years an English possession. There were many French there who
had no great love for England, and they wished
the Americans success. The address of Congress to the American people was received
throughout the colonies with the greatest enthusiasm. It was indorsed in the colonial assemblies as their own sentiments, and thanks
were offered to their delegates who had so wisely and prudently represented them. They also

resolved that if the king and parliament did not retrace their steps and retire within the bounds of the British constitution, so dear to British subjects in America as well as in England, that they would resist their unlawful and tyrannical decrees by every means in their power.

"Notice, children, just where the difficulty lay. It was not British rule or constitutional law that our fathers resisted; it was King George the Third and his ministers and parliament, who attempted to overstep the limits of their powers and tyrannize over loyal British subjects. The address to the people of England as fellow-countrymen was very well received. The city of London and other parts of the kingdom sent up petitions to the British authorities in favor of the American cause; for the English people had suffered themselves in time past from the tyranny of their kings—so much so that they had rebelled and taken up arms. You remember they had brought King Charles the First to the block and taken off his head, and afterward they rose in wrath against King James and drove him from the throne.

"Of all the members of a nation or government, it is certainly most befitting that the king, or the head of the nation whatever be his title, should sacredly observe the laws himself if he would have loyal subjects. Very many of the English people sided with the Americans and wished them success. Many learned and eminent men addressed letters to the king and the ministers against their unwise course. In parliament, too, many of the noblest and most eloquent of British statesmen pleaded their cause ; while the greatest of them all, the eloquent old man Chatham, bending beneath the weight of years, his keen and vigorous intellect undimmed by the touch of time, appeared once more in the House of Lords, to denounce the blindness and madness of Lord North, the ministry, and King George, and to eulogize the American cause as set forth by the statesmen of the American Congress. These words closed his speech : 'For myself I must avow that in all my reading—and I have read Thucydides, and studied and admired the master statesmen of the world—for solidity of reason, force of sagacity, and wisdom of conclusion under a complication of difficult circumstances, no nation or body of men can stand in preference to the General Congress of Philadelphia. The histories of Greece and Rome give us nothing equal to it, and all attempts to impose servitude upon such a mighty continental nation must be vain. If the ministers persevere in thus misleading the king, I will not say that the king is betrayed, but I will pronounce that the kingdom is undone ; I will not say that they can alienate the affections of his subjects from his crown, but I will affirm that, the American jewel out of it, they will make the crown not worth his wearing.'

"The eloquence of the friends of America availed nothing. They were outvoted ; the respectful and dignified petitions of the Congress were spurned with contempt, and the inhabitants of Massachusetts were declared 'rebels.' Across the channel France looked on and smiled, well pleased at England's madness and folly. She was working out that ruin for herself which France had so long desired to see. Meantime all over the hills and through the valleys of our land the 'Sons of Liberty' and the 'Minute Men' were calling to arms, gathering together what powder and cannon could be found, brightening their firelocks, organizing and drilling. In Massachusetts they slept on their arms, had no faith in British promises and less fear of British threats.

"General Gage's fleet rode idly at anchor in Boston harbor. British troops had fortified the adjacent hills, and men held their breath and waited to know 'What next ?' At Concord, a day's march away from Boston, the Massachusetts rebels had stored cannon and arms. General Gage was informed of it, and planned an excursion thither to seize it. The soldiers were to start at night to avoid suspicion and make it a surprise. But the patriots of Boston had their eyes and ears open, and two hours in advance of their time Dr. Warren, a 'high Son of Liberty,' dispatched two trusty Minute Men on the road to Concord to sound the alarm and call up the militia. Soon every farm-house was astir, the village bells rang, and beacon-lights streamed out. At Lexington the Minute Men assembled and paraded, and after waiting several hours a watch was set, and they were dismissed with orders to assemble at drum-beat. The last stars faded back into the sky as the drum-call was again heard through the village. It was promptly obeyed. Seventy men answered to their names and took station on the village green, close beside the meeting-house and hard by the village grave-yard, where slept the sacred dust of their fathers, who had loved their liberties more than their lives. They stood silent and fearless. It had been better, perhaps, if they had made no stand at Lexington, but had fallen back to Concord and swelled the numbers at the threatened point ; but they thought best to stand by their own homes and altars. There they stood on that sweet spring morning, April 19, 1775. Jonas Parker, 'the strongest and best wrestler in Lexington, had vowed never to run from British troops, and he kept it.' The British, seven companies strong, infantry and grenadiers, came up at double-quick, calling out, 'Disperse, ye rebels! Ye rebels, lay down your arms!' The Americans stood still, and the British order was given, 'Fire!' They fired, and the dying and the wounded lay stretched on the village green. Jonas Parker, seeing that it would be murder, not battle, with seventy against seven hundred, ordered his men to retire. As they did so they answered the enemy's fire at random. The British continued still to fire, killing and wounding. One of their murderous balls brought Jonas Parker to his knees. He had discharged his gun and was reloading, 'when as brave a heart as ever beat for freedom was stilled by a bayonet, and he lay on the post which he took at the morning drum-beat.'

"The British drew up on the green, now crimson with warm life-blood, fired a volley, sent up three huzzas for the brilliant victory, and marched on toward Concord. At two o'clock that morning the drum had roused the

militia. They assembled, two hundred strong—
a band of neighbors, brothers, known to each
other in their daily walks and toils, and meeting at the same altar for worship. Their minister stood with them, his gun on his shoulder.
His sermons and prayers had nerved their
hearts and hands to the sacred duty of defending their civil liberties ; for, losing these, how
long would they enjoy religious liberty ? Finding themselves largely outnumbered, they fell
back north of the town to wait for reinforcements. The British entered Concord at sun-
rise, spiked a few cannon, and threw into the
river all the powder they could find, the greater
part having been removed ; they then employed
themselves with plundering private property.
Before long, however, their cavalry, which had
been scouring the country, returned with the
news of a general uprising and gathering of
militia, and advised that they turn their faces
with all speed toward Boston."

"Ha! ha!" said Albert. "From Boston to
Concord was a good move, no doubt, but from
Concord to Boston is another thing."

"While they deliberated the American militia
approached the bridge, led by one Isaac Davis.
The British began to pull up the planks, seeing
which the Americans quickened their step,

They had been charged to wait for the enemy's fire. Before they reached the bridge a volley was poured into their brave ranks, and Isaac Davis fell dead. 'Just thirty-three years old, father of four little ones, stately in person, a man of few words, earnest even to solemnity, he parted from his wife, saying, "Take good care of the children." She gazed after him with resignation as he led his company to the scene of danger. That afternoon he was carried home and laid in her bedroom. His countenance was little altered and was pleasant in death. God gave her length of days in the land which his generous self-devotion assisted to redeem. She lived to see her country touch the Gulf of Mexico and the Pacific, and when it was grown great in numbers, wealth, and power, the United States, in Congress, paid honors to her husband's martyrdom.' Isaac Davis' townsmen pressed on to do their duty. Command to fire was given, and the British ranks broke in confusion, leaving the bridge with those to whom it belonged. The Americans followed up their advantage, fresh recruits pouring in at every step of the way. The British, wearied with their long march and encumbered with their wounded, could make but slow time. The Americans trod uncomfortably upon their heels,

and the fire waxed hotter. From behind every
tree and stone fence the bullets whistled, partic-.
ular attention being paid to the officers. Maddened to terror by their seen and unseen foes
the retreat became a rout, and they fled through
Lexington in hot haste. There were no tri-
umphant huzzas now. They would have been
utterly destroyed, but they were met by Lord
Percy with twelve hundred fresh troops and
two pieces of artillery. He formed a hollow
square and let the fugitives lie down to rest,
panting, with 'their tongues hanging out of their
mouths, like dogs after a chase,' while his artillery kept the Americans at bay for awhile. The
Minute Men, however, continued to gather, and
the cry was 'still they come.' Lord Percy knew
his position was perilous and pushed on as
rapidly as possible. The unerring rebel marks-
men now on his flanks, now on his rear, terrified
the troops again into rout. In vain the officers
threatened and ordered. The men ran like
sheep; nor could they be brought to order
again until they found themselves safe under
the guns of the fleet, with the loss of three hundred killed, wounded, and missing, among whom
were many officers. Above all, they had to
lament the loss of honor and prestige. The
king's regulars had been driven in disgrace be-

fore these rebel 'rogues and rascals,' who had been represented as too mean-spirited to fight ; of whom it had been promised in parliament that any British general with five regiments of infantry could traverse the whole country and drive the inhabitants from one end to the other. The mortification of General Gage was extreme.

"The militia did not return to their homes, but took post near Boston, cutting off all supplies, and the king's army and fleet found themselves beleaguered in their turn. They continued to gather in the camp until their numbers swelled to thirty thousand men, who only waited the orders of Congress to drive the British into the sea, or at least to attempt it."

"Hurra! turn about's fair play," cried Harry as the second tea-bell rang ; and taking Stevey on his back, he carried him three times round the room and bore him triumphantly in to the supper-table.

CHAPTER XI.

Eaton and Allen—Bunker Hill—Second Congress—
General George Washington.

"￼OME, aunty, the clock is just going to strike six, and we are anxious to know what the people said when they heard about Lexington and Concord."

"Well, Nannie, I'll borrow a paragraph by way of reply," said Aunt Edith, turning the leaves of a volume of Bancroft. She read: "Heralds on swift relays of horses transmitted the war-message from hand to hand, till village repeated it to village, the sea to the backwoods, the plains to the highlands, till it had been borne north, south, east, and west. It broke the rest of the trappers of New Hampshire, and, ringing like bugle-notes from peak to peak, overleaped the Green Mountains, swept onward to Montreal, and descended the ocean river to the cliffs of Quebec. The hills along the Hudson told to one another the tale. As the summons hurried south it was one day at New York; in one more at Philadelphia; the next it lighted a watch-fire at Baltimore; thence it waked an answer at Annapolis. Crossing the

10

Potomac near Mount Vernon, it was sent forward to Williamsburgh. Still onward, through the boundless groves of evergreen, to Wilmington, North Carolina. Patriots of South Carolina caught up its tones and dispatched it to Charleston, and through pines, and palmettoes, and moss-clad live-oaks, still further south beyond the Savannah. The Blue Ridge took up the voice and made it heard through the Valley of Virginia; the Alleghanies, as they listened, opened their barriers that the 'loud call' might pass through to the hardy riflemen on the Holston and the French Broad. It breathed its inspiring word to the first settlers of Kentucky, and the hunters in the watchless valley of the Elkhorn named their encampment Lexington."

"Isn't that grand!" said Harry, waving his handkerchief with one hand and gesticulating with the other.

"O, certainly," said Albert. "You mean, 'Give me liberty or give me death!'"

"Yes, that's it. I'm obliged to you. That's my present sentiments."

"You are entirely welcome, Mr. Buncombe. Now, please, come to order." Aunt Edith continued: "New England had silently in her heart declared war, and Yankee invention was busy as to the best way of making it. The men of Connecticut, looking northward toward Canada, reflected that England would without doubt plan a rear attack upon them by way of that province. How would they come, Albert ?"

" Down Lakes Champlain and George to the Hudson River, I suppose."

" Yes, right into the very heart of the colonies. This was very much to be dreaded. When France owned Canada she had fortified two points between the Lakes George and Champlain ; whoever held these posts commanded the pass into the colonies. The English had won them by hard fighting from the French, and they were now held by small garrisons of English soldiers. The assembly of Connecticut reflected that in the event of a war these garrisons would be strengthened by fresh forces, and in secret council they determined to send a detachment to seize those places at once, especially as they contained large quantities of arms and cannon, of which the Americans had great need. The assembly therefore voted one thousand eight hundred dollars to defray the expenses of the expedition, and appointed Colonels Eaton and Allen to command it. Not a moment was to be lost. The troops assembled on the shore of Lake George. Albert, you can show the children the course by your map.

They were mostly from Vermont, and were called 'Green Mountain Boys'—hardy fellows who had slept many a time on 'a bear-skin, with a roll of snow for a pillow.' They posted sentinels, who were charged to observe strict silence. Rapid marching brought them to the lake-shore, opposite the fortress of Ticonderoga, one nightfall. They did not sleep, but employed the night in crossing the lake with muffled oars. At gray dawn they scaled the walls, and sent up a shout of triumph on the still morning air. They seized the guns from the hands of the astonished sentinels ; there was a short scuffle and the garrison submitted. The commander appeared, rubbing his sleepy eyes, and, to his inquiry, 'What does this mean?' Colonel Allen replied, 'You are the prisoner of America.' 'By what authority?' pleaded the officer. 'In the name of the great Jehovah and the Continental Congress,' answered Allen. This was on the tenth of May, 1775.

"The Green Mountain Boys did not tarry long, but advanced to Crown Point and took it in the same unceremonious manner. They seized the only English war-vessel at that time on the lake, and going down the lake to Wood Creek took a small fort named Skeenesborough. Besides the possession of these important points, which they garrisoned, they obtained one hundred and twenty pieces of cannon, besides mortars and ammunition of all kinds, part of which they dragged overland to the camp before Boston, where it was much needed. The British army and fleet now began to be straitened for provisions. The American farmers would not sell to them, and the American soldiers watched them so closely that they could not steal any thing. Their stores were exhausted ; it was a long distance to bring one's dinner, three thousand miles across the ocean, often against contrary winds and tides."

"What a pity King George didn't consider that before he undertook this war !" exclaimed Albert.

"Unfortunately, King George was not the only king who forgot the Scripture admonition to count the cost before going upon a warfare. But to continue. The reinforcements they had been expecting from England had now arrived, in charge of three of the most distinguished generals the British army could boast—Generals Howe, Clinton, and Burgoyne. They had at command ten thousand well-disciplined English regulars. The shame of Lexington and Concord remained to be wiped from the British name ; moreover it was becoming necessary to

break through the American lines to obtain
forage and provisions for their army. An attack was planned by the officers, but upon
reconnoitering their positions the Americans
were found so strongly posted, and standing so
well upon their guard, that the British general
declined to risk a failure, which would be very
depressing to his cause at this time. He contented himself with standing upon the defensive. Not so the Americans. They continued
to advance and fortify. One 'sun-down,' unperceived by the British, they took possession
of a hill that commanded both the city and harbor of Boston. All the night through, the brave
New Englanders plied their picks and spades,
and by daybreak had constructed quite a strong
earthwork. About five o'clock in the morning
the commander of one of the war-vessels perceived the mischievous work, and ordered his
artillery to play upon it. This roused the officers. Looking through their glasses, they could
scarcely believe their own eyes. If it came to
successful completion they would be compelled
to leave Boston themselves, instead of driving
away the Americans. They promptly ordered
the artillery of the city, the fleet, and all the
floating batteries to a furious fire, notwithstanding which, the Americans continued industri-

ously dodging and digging all day long. At
night, the enemy's fire lacked aim and did little
damage, while the Americans did much work.
By morning the earthen fort was formidable,
and the British general ordered an assault.
Bunker's Hill stood just outside of Charlestown,
a village of wooden houses. This village was
ordered to be set on fire, that the troops might
advance to the assault with more safety under
cover of the smoke. They came up slowly and
cautiously, the flames of the burning town not
helping them at all, as an 'ill wind' blew the
smoke where it was not wanted. The Americans, having no powder to waste, waited till the
British were well in reach, then leveling their
muskets for slow and sure aim they sent their
first discharge into the advancing lines. Reloading quickly they sent another. It was too
hot for British courage ; they wavered and fell
back in confusion, the ground strewed thickly
with the dead and wounded. Their officers ran
hither and thither with promises, orders, and
threats. At last they rallied them, and once
more they advanced to the assault. The same
scene was repeated ; they could not stand such
a storm of well-sent bullets, and this time they
retreated back to their boats. But General
Howe, seeing the ill-fortune of the day, had

hastened to lead fresh reinforcements to their support. With desperate efforts the men rallied for a third attack, which was well planned, and led in person by General Howe. The powder of the Americans was at the last charge; they delivered it, and for awhile after beat back the British lines with the butt-end of their muskets. Meantime a furious fire from all the guns of the fleet had broken and uncovered their earthworks, besides making it impossible for any reinforcements of men or powder to reach them. They had done all that men could do, and the signal of retreat was given. They made an admirable and orderly retreat, and escaped with little loss as they had fought behind intrenchments.

"The victory was dearly bought by the English. Their loss in men and officers was frightful; they were unable to pursue the Americans, and thus the victory was a barren and unprofitable one. The brave defense made and the little loss suffered by the Americans left the glory with them, while the position gained was only one more point to defend, and brought no positive advantage to the British cause. From Bunker's Hill, June 17, 1775, the question was answered whether or not the Americans could and would fight. This answer was duly reported by General Howe to the British Parliament and King George.

"Meantime the second American Congress had convened at Philadelphia in May, and were forced to recognize the Revolution as begun and the country at war with England. They still disclaimed any intention of independence or separation from the mother country, but declared their firm purpose of maintaining their rights with arms in their hands. They added, however, that whenever the king and parliament would signify their willingness to repeal all their tyrannical and unreasonable acts, and give them guarantees for the future, at that moment they would lay down their arms."

"Pshaw!" said Harry, contemptuously, "what was the use of wasting their valuable time powwowing with a simpleton like King George?"

"Softly, my boy; it becomes the dignity of a great nation, carrying the destinies of millions, always to act slowly and deliberately. Haste, impulse, we can forgive in the individual, but not in the nation. The fathers were wise men. They knew that a good cause can always bide its time and lose nothing by so doing. Some of them—eagle-eyed, far-sighted men, like Samuel Adams, of Massachusetts, and Thomas Jefferson, of Virginia;· men of intuition like

Patrick Henry, and Gadsden, of South Carolina—doubtless saw the end from the beginning; but the many did not—indeed, were not ready for it. Revolutions always accomplish more than their leaders intend. Men start revolutions and then cannot arrest them. God shapes their ends to his high purposes. Virginia, New England, Pennsylvania, Maryland, and South Carolina were in advance of some of the other colonies. Our fathers thought it was well to wait until the others came up with them in opinion. They must move abreast with one heart and one step. They adopted 'new views' as soon as they recognized them as the 'true views' for the hour. Nevertheless, they did at this time exercise the sovereign powers of a nation. They established a general post-office system from Maine to Georgia; they prepared a currency and issued bills of credit to defray the national expenses; they organized a continental army, to be composed of regiments recruited in all the various colonies, and elected George Washington, of Virginia, commander-in-chief of the American army."

"Hail to the Chief!" said Albert, bowing low.

"See, the conquering hero comes!" echoed Harry.

"Now we'll not want for a hero," added Nannie, "all the rest of the way."

"I don't think we have wanted for one yet," said Stevey.

"Do you know any thing about him, my little Stevey," said Aunt Edith.

"Not much," answered the child, "but I think you told me once about little George, a brave boy who never told a lie."

"The very same, Stevey. He was grown to manhood now. His country trusted him above all his fellows. She called him to her altar, placed her hopes, her liberties, and her destinies in his hands, and charged him to keep them safe from harm. He had grown up without masters, and with little learning except what he had acquired himself. Two facts in his boyhood I want you to notice. Whatever he undertook of study, play, or work was thoroughly, faithfully done, up to its highest capability. He kept the society of the wisest and best people he could find. He held himself loftily, even as a boy; there was something grand and kingly in his air and manner, as if some vision of his future station mingled with his boyish dreams. The truthfulness of boyhood ripened into the integrity of manhood, until it became the law of his nature; so that one says of him, 'a planet would sooner have shot from its sphere than he have departed from his uprightness.' He prized and loved truth above all else, and gave himself to its service with a single eye. Here the words

WASHINGTON.

of the Divine Master find a fulfillment: 'If thine eye be single, thy whole body shall be full of light.' Washington approached as near to infallibility as it is possible for humanity to do. He made few mistakes; clear and far-sighted, he saw what was best to be done, how much it was possible to do, and did not attempt the impossible. Other men were brave as he, still others were more learned than he, or endowed with more conspicuous gifts, but none were so wise, so skillful, so sure, so unerring. His eye was single, his aim was single. He lived to serve the truth, and the God of truth gave him light without measure. His whole being, all his faculties, stood in divine illumination. Children, he honored God by trusting him ; in the darkest hour of his country's fortunes he never despaired. He believed her cause was just, and that the God of justice would ordain her triumph in his own good time. All the world came to believe in and honor Washington. It is remarked that no man who ever lived 'had in so great a degree the faculty to command the confidence of his fellow-men and rule the willing. Wherever he became known—in his family, in his neighborhood, his county, his native State, the whole continent, in camp, in civil life, among the common people, in foreign courts, throughout the civilized world, and even among savages —he, beyond all other men, had the confidence of his kind.'

" He had been for many years in the military service of his native State, and had won good reputation as a soldier—his name, indeed, had crossed the ocean, and he was spoken of at the

British court as 'the brave Colonel Washington.'
In the French War he had served under British
officers. He was with Bradddock, who suffered
a disastrous defeat because he was too proud to
take young Colonel Washington's advice, and
after Braddock's death Washington's skill preserved and brought off the army from what
seemed utter destruction. Indeed, Washington,
all through his career, showed his highest genius in repairing the errors of others, and saving
a cause in spite of the mistakes of its friends
and the assaults of its enemies. He did not
seek the high honor that was conferred on him,
neither did he desire it. He accepted it as a
duty. He well knew the toils and perils that
lay before him, that inevitably joined themselves
to this office. He was a man of few words;
modest as he was brave ; noble in form and
feature, eyes of blue, tender in expression, even
to sadness, they say. Patrick Henry, who sat
beside him when it was announced that the
vote electing him was unanimous, says that a
tear glistened in his eye as he rose from his
seat, and, after refusing all pay beyond his expenses, said, 'As the Congress desire it I will
enter upon the momentous duty, and exert
every power I possess in their service and for
the support of the glorious cause. But I beg it

may be remembered by every gentleman in the
room that I this day declare, with the utmost
sincerity, I do not think myself equal to the
command I am honored with.'

" His instructions were to repair immediately
to the camp before Boston. At a farewell
supper the members of Congress rose as they
drank a health ' to the commander-in-chief of
the American army ;' to his thanks they listened in silence, for the sense of the difficulties
which lay before him suppressed every festal
cheer. To his wife, whose miniature he wore
on his heart from the day of his marriage to his
death, he wrote saying, ' I hope my undertaking
this service is designed to answer a good purpose. I rely confidently on Providence.' His
journey to Boston was a triumphal procession.
Arriving in camp, he was met with affectionate
welcome by all the officers. Trumbull, governor
of Connecticut, wrote him : 'Now be strong
and very courageous, and the God of the armies
of Israel give you wisdom and fortitude, and
cover your head in the day of battle.'

" Congress continued its deliberations. It
recommended to each colony that all men able
to bear arms, between the ages of sixteen and
fifty, should be enrolled in companies, furnish
themselves with arms, and exercise in their use.

Every-where the request became a law, and
was obeyed with alacrity. Our Revolutionary
mothers with their own hands embroidered the
colors with patriotic mottoes, and presented
them to the regiments with words of encouragement. They were also advised to foster the
manufacture of all materials and implements of
war, for war was now the business of the nation.
What was no less important, the Congress applied themselves to establish and give shape
and permanence to their own authority, as the
visible executor of the will of the American
people. For this purpose they drew up what
they called 'Articles of Confederation of the
United Colonies of America.' While each colony was to preserve its authority over its own
local concerns, this congress of their deputies
was to exercise supreme authority in all that
concerned the general interests of all the colonies. For instance, Congress was to make
war or peace for all; contract alliances and
hold intercourse with foreign nations; regulate
commerce; control the mint; direct the movements of the army in council with its general-in-
chief; and appoint all the officers of the continental army and foreign embassadors. No single
colony had the right to do these things. The
expenses of the war and of the Congress were

to be paid from a public treasury, which was to be filled from each colony according to the number of its male inhabitants. There was also elected a council of twelve which should execute all the laws of Congress when that body was not in session ; for in time of war there always occur sudden emergencies that must be met at the moment—vexing questions that must have immediate answer. These articles were submitted to the different colonies for their approval. Congress also ordered that a detachment of the army under Generals Schuyler and Montgomery should invade Canada, taking possession of Montreal and Quebec, and invite the Canadians to join them in resisting British tyranny. This might be called a measure of defense, because the British General Carleton was endeavoring to enlist the Canadians to invade our territory and retake the Forts Ticonderoga and Crown Point."

11

CHAPTER XII.

The Canadian Expedition—Richard Montgomery.

" ALL aboard for Canada!" was Harry's salutation this evening. Albert had wheeled up the lounge toward Aunt Edith, so that Stevey might lie comfortably and listen. Little Grace was curled up at the other end of the lounge with her kitten in her lap, for she had learned to sit quite still while the talk flowed over her young head.

"All aboard for Canada!" repeated Aunt Edith. "We can easily say that, Harry, beside this bright winter fire, with our comfortable surroundings ; wait until I draw the picture of our brave Revolutionary soldiers marching barefoot and half-clothed through Canadian snow-drifts, and we shall be able to measure the long distance between reading or talking about heroes and being heroes ourselves. Generals Schuyler and Montgomery were ordered to assemble their forces at a point on Lake Champlain. Here General Schuyler fell ill and was obliged to return home, leaving the expedition, its dangers and glories, to the youthful Mont-

9607.

Montgomery's Expedition into Canada.

gomery. He was a man of great military experience for his years ; full of gifts, graces, and accomplishments ; one of the most admired and beloved of the Revolutionary heroes. The order to take charge of the Canadian expedition reached him in his beautiful home on the banks of the Hudson, where with his young wife, whom he tenderly loved, he had settled, hoping for quiet years of domestic happiness in a home adorned with every refinement. But Montgomery loved honor more than life, and liberty more than happiness. He obeyed the call of his country. Albert, take your map and show the children the Sorel River, which joins Lake Champlain and the River St. Lawrence. Do you see any forts named there ?"

" Yes, aunty," said Nannie, " Fort St. John and Fort Chambly."

" Since the Americans had taken Forts Ticonderoga and Crown Point the English had much strengthened these forts, especially St. John, as they were the only remaining defenses of Canada on that line. It was necessary to take it by siege. As soon as Montgomery's little band, not more than one thousand in number, were armed and equipped, their gallant commander led them on until they came near Fort St. John, when they proceeded to invest it."

"What does that mean, aunty?" asked little Alice.

"Albert, will you tell us how it is done?"

"Sometimes by taking positions on hills or eminences outside the fort and mounting cannon to bear on it, sometimes by digging trenches until approaches are made near enough to make a final assault."

"Yes, that's it. This fort was well armed and garrisoned, and its capture was a work of time. Hearing that Fort St. John was thus closely besieged, the British General Carleton came with a large force, intending to engage Montgomery in battle outside and thus relieve the fort, or, as military men call it, raise the siege. But Montgomery was ready to receive him. Carleton suffered a defeat and retreated with great loss. Montgomery proceeded with the siege. Fort Chambly being feebly garrisoned, he had dispatched a small number who surprised and captured it; this afforded him a further supply of cannon and ammunition. The provisions of the garrison of St. John were now nearly exhausted. Montgomery's trenches were near enough for the assault; he therefore sent a summons to the commander to surrender and thus save further bloodshed, informing him also of Carleton's defeat. Seeing no hope of succor from any quarter, he accepted Montgomery's terms and surrendered the post. The colors taken from the English were presented to Congress. Leaving a garrison to hold the fort, Montgomery hastened on toward Montreal. So rapid were his movements and so well-planned his attack, that General Carleton, after a slight resistance, fled in disguise to Quebec. The city capitulated, and many vessels and naval stores fell to the victors. Montgomery's object was to make friends of the Canadians and induce them to join the cause of the Colonies. Though they did not do this, yet they received the Americans kindly, and supplied them and their army with all that they needed. The news of this brilliant train of victories spread over the land. Montgomery's praises were on every tongue, and Congress voted him the thanks of the nation. But the young soldier's heart was sad. After leaving garrisons at Chambly, St. John, and Montreal, he found himself with only three hundred effective men left him to attempt the capture of Quebec, which was, by natural position and military art, the most strongly fortified city in America. A Canadian winter was upon them, and their perils and hardships had but just commenced. Sad presentiments chilled Montgomery's heart. He often thought of his peaceful home in the bosom of the hills, the loving wife sitting in her loneliness there. He would have bartered all the glory he had won for one hour at that hearthstone. Should he ever see it again?

"Washington had forseen the situation in which Montgomery would find himself, and, knowing that without the capture of Quebec the expedition (the object of which was the conquest of Canada) would be a failure, had dispatched a column from his own camp near Boston to penetrate the State of Maine and come out into Canada at Quebec. He even hoped that they would reach it in time to surprise and take it while Montgomery was operating against Montreal. If not, they were to await his coming and operate with him. This force consisted of ten companies of New England infantry, one of Virginia riflemen under the brave Morgan, and two companies of Pennsylvanians. In all the records of ancient or modern valor I have read nothing equal to this wrestle of heroism and endurance with toil and suffering. Let us follow these noble soldiers on the map. They were to sail up the Kennebec River as far as navigable, then they were to take flat-boats, which Washington had ordered to be constructed for their use ; thence up the Dead River, a branch of the Kennebec. After that their path lay through an uninhabited wilderness until they came to the sources of the Canadian River, called the Chaudiere, which empties itself into the St. Lawrence River quite near Quebec."

" It looks tolerably easy by the map," said Albert.

" Yes, by the map ; but as they advanced up the Kennebec the stream became rapid and violent over its rocky bed ; often they could not row, but had to drag their heavily-laden boats up the swift current, waist deep. It was winter, remember ; the mountains were covered with snow and the waters at a deadly chill. Beds of rock, falls and rapids, often forbade the passage of their boats at all. They had to be unloaded, arms, ammunition, baggage and provisions, and the boats themselves carried by the men through tiresome pathless forests until the stream would bear their boats again. Leaving the Kennebec, they dragged every thing over a rough mountain-ridge and through swamps and bogs, sinking knee-deep, to the Dead River. Their course now lay up this river for eighty-three miles, and no less than seventeen times, because of falls and rapids,

they were forced to unload their boats and
carry them, as I have before described. Winter winds howled around them ; their shoes
were gone ; briers and rocks had torn their
clothes from their backs ; storms drenched
them ; they had no shelter at night, except
what they made with the boughs of trees ;
their provisions were nearly gone ; famine and
death marched with them, until they were
forced to kill their faithful dogs that had followed their masters' steps into the wilderness.
But the love of liberty and their country kept
its flame alive on the altar of their hearts and
they toiled on. They had dragged their boats
one hundred and eighty miles of the journey ;
they had carried them on their shoulders with
all their contents, forty miles, through frightful
thickets, ragged mountains, and knee-deep bogs,
till at last they reached the Chaudiere, which
goes foaming down its rocky bed at too rapid a
speed ; for it whirled over three of their boats,
and they lost much of the stores and ammunition which they had brought so far with so
much labor. They were nearing their journey's end, and the first French Canadians who
saw them wondered if they had fallen from the
clouds. Arnold had sent forward several letters to Montgomery by the hands of friendly

Indians to apprise him of his coming. Unfortunately, these letters were intercepted."

"O don't tell us that," said Harry, with a world of vexation in his face.

"Yes, but for this it was very possible that Arnold's brave heroes, worn and tattered as they were, coming suddenly upon the garrison, might have surprised and carried the defenses of the city; but the British strengthened their works and stood well upon their guard. Arnold bravely offered them battle outside the fort, but they did not accept it, and he was forced to march away some miles and wait for Montgomery's arrival. It was a glad day when their eyes caught the first sight of the American colors borne by Montgomery's men. There was a joyful meeting of friends in that far-off winter-land. Montgomery had brought them woolen clothing and boots; he also gave them words of cheer and encouragement for their almost superhuman achievements. Counting their little band, those who remained to Montgomery after battle, siege, and assault, and those who remained to Arnold from the perils of the wilderness, they amounted to a few less than one thousand, including two companies of Canadians. This handful of men appeared in mid-winter before Quebec, defended by two hundred pieces of cannon and a garrison of twice their number, well provisioned. Montgomery spoke hopefully to his men, but in his heart he carried a weight of despair. To return without taking Quebec was to throw away all the brave work he had done. Congress expected it ; the nation waited for it. A soldier's fame is dear to him as life ; to a patriot the cause of his country is above all else. No time was to be lost ; the rigors of winter were becoming intolerable, and the sufferings of the men were beyond endurance. Two diseases attacked the camp, small-pox and homesickness."

" Poor fellows !" said Nannie, the tears standing in her eyes. " Dear aunty, what *did* put it into their heads to go in the winter ? "

" Sure enough," added Albert. " You said Washington never made mistakes, but that seemed very much like one."

" They did not choose the winter, but they accepted it as a necessity. England had no army in Canada at this time, in the spring she would have. It was now or never for the capture of Canada ; moreover, Congress ordered the Canadian expedition ; being ordered, Washington contributed to the best of his ability to its success. Montgomery and Arnold used every honorable provocation to induce General Carleton to come out of his defenses and fight; they would then have had a fair chance of success. But the British general thought 'prudence the better part of valor.' Finding all his efforts unavailing, Montgomery said, ' To the storming we must come at last.'

" The year was growing old, but a few days remaining of 1775. The term of enlistment of most of the men expired with it. The generals planned for a night assault. ' The night of the 26th of December was clear, and so cold that no man could handle his arms or scale a wall. The 27th was hazy, and the troops were put in motion ; but the sky cleared, and Montgomery, tender of their lives, called them back and waited for a night of clouds and darkness, with a storm of wind and snow.'

" On the thirtieth, the New Year's eve, a north-east snow-storm set in. The troops were divided for attack at different points, Montgomery reserving the post of danger for himself. Two of the attacks were to be mere pretenses, to draw attention from the real points, which were to be assaulted by Arnold on one side and Montgomery on the other. The snow had changed to driving hail that cut the men's eyes and faces ; they advanced with heads down and their guns under their coats to keep them dry. A braver man than Arnold never led men to battle. They assailed their point of attack with the greatest fury. A musket-ball in his leg disabled Arnold early in the action, and he was borne to the rear. Morgan took command, and cheering on his men with words of victory, they carried the battery and took its defenders prisoners, though with great loss of life. He held for a time the lower part of the town, and there they waited and watched for the promised signals from Montgomery's side.

"He with three hundred men and his two aids, MacPherson and Cheeseman, two gallant young soldiers, took their course along a steep and rocky path, made so slippery and dangerous by the frozen snow and hail that it was a constant effort to keep their feet. On they went, Montgomery opening the path through the snow with his own hands. A battery intercepted their path—it must be taken. Montgomery ordered them to 'double-quick,' himself leading, with the words, 'Come on, brave boys, you will not fear to follow where your general leads.' A flash, a 'well-served cannon dis-·charge,' Montgomery, MacPherson, and Cheeseman fall dead. The drifted snow was the winding-sheet of the beautiful and brave on the morning of the New Year 1776, before the gates of Quebec. Seeing their leaders fall, the men had no courage to advance over their dead bodies. They retreated. Morgan and his men waited on the other side of the town for the signals, which, alas! they should never see. They waited too long. The enemy, released from defending other points, surrounded and took them prisoners. To General Carleton's praise be it spoken, the bodies of the noble fallen received burial with all the honors of war. Montgomery had fought under England's banner in his youth, and had even then won a name for honor and valor. When the news of his death reached England, the 'great defenders of liberty in the British Parliament vied with each other in his praise,' and wept as they pronounced his eulogy. Washington bewailed his loss, for he loved him as a brother. All over the land men wept as for a 'heart friend.' Congress, 'desiring to transmit to future ages an example of patriotism, boldness of enterprise, and contempt of danger and death, reared a monument of marble to the glory of Richard Montgomery.'

"But the bitterest tears were shed in that pleasant home amid the hills of Hudson; a grief was there for which earth had no balm, for Montgomery's wife took no other love in his stead. Years after the toils of war had passed, Washington kept state in the city of New York as first President of the Republic for which Montgomery had *died*, and for which Washington had *lived.* It is related

RICHARD MONTGOMERY.

that on reception-days 'it was the custom for the secretaries and gentlemen of the household to hand ladies to and from their carriages ; but when the honored widow of Montgomery came, the President himself performed these complimentary duties.'"

The little group sat silent for a moment, and

Albert said, "I can't help thinking, aunty, that it was a great mistake for them to undertake this expedition."

"If we consider it as a piece of offensive warfare, perhaps it was, though the cause of failure seemed to be the accident of Montgomery's death at the critical moment ; for it was afterward found that the battery was served only by a handful of men, and if Montgomery had not fallen its capture would have been an easy matter. He without whom the sparrow does not fall gave the final orders. We 'rough hew' our destinies, but He 'shapes' them as he wills. It would doubtless have been better if they had stood upon their defense, instead of entering a neutral province, and had contented themselves with putting strong garrisons into the forts on the Lakes, on our own territory, thus keeping the doors into Canada well locked on this side. No success attended them afterward, though Congress, against Washington's advice, continued their efforts to accomplish their designs there. War is a horrible wickedness, and includes every form of suffering and wrong. It is unmitigated barbarism from beginning to end, except in defense of a just cause. In that case we are commanded to 'resist unto blood,' and every man who lays down his life fairly earns the name of martyr.

"Montgomery gave his life to win for us those civil and religious liberties which have made our country 'the glory of all lands.' The hero keeps his quiet, unbroken slumber in the grave-yard of St. Paul's Church, New York, just a step aside from Broadway. Of all the busy, toiling, hurrying millions that yearly pass and repass above the sacred dust, how many pause to lay upon his grave the chaplet of a grateful memory?"

CHAPTER XIII.

King George's Troops ask Washington's Leave to go out of Boston—The British next pay their Respects to Charleston, and are Inhospitably Received by Moultrie behind Palmetto Logs.

" ET us visit this evening, children, the camp near Boston, where Washington had remained apparently inactive, though not really so. The terms of enlistment of most of the men had expired, and he had in fact recruited and disciplined a new army. This sore evil of short enlistments was one of the chief difficulties that beset Washington at every step throughout the war, and which he never could prevail on Congress altogether to remedy. For months the farmers of New England had fed this army by contributions. This, however, could not last. Washington had organized his army in its commissariat, though the want of money still left it far from perfect. Worst of all, they lacked ammunition, particularly powder, of which they had only about one hundred barrels. This fact the General was most careful to conceal, lest their

12

enemies should avail themselves of it; and though Congress had more than once signified its desire that the army should assume the offensive, yet Washington was obliged to remain inactive, without giving the cause of his inactivity, and was thus compelled to stand open to the censure of his countrymen. He was simply waiting for the auspicious moment, more careful of the cause he served than of his own reputation. The British army was nine thousand strong, comfortably stowed in winter-quarters in Boston city, chiefly busy in inventing amusements for passing the time. They had established a riding-school in the old South Meeting-house, and a theater in Faneuil Hall, where the officers appeared as actors on the stage. They had no thought of danger and expected to stay until spring, when they were to take possession of New York by the aid of large reinforcements brought from England. Washington had thus far failed to draw them out of their intrenchments for open battle; his own force and military supplies were not sufficient to warrant him in attacking them behind their works. In council with his officers, it was at last decided to take possession of Dorchester Hills, south of Boston, and fortify them. This would compel them either

to come out and fight or to evacuate the city
and harbor.

" The night appointed was favorable. Preparations down to the minutest detail had been
completed. Every man knew his place and
his task. Washington had, for two nights
previously, ordered a cannonade of the town
in order to divert attention. This night the
bombardment was as furious as they could
make it ; they wanted all the noise possible.
A party of eight hundred as guard led the procession to the heights ; next followed twelve
hundred workmen with carts full of intrench-
ing tools. The ground was frozen too hard to
afford earth defenses, but the General had provided for this. A train of three hundred carts
were coming and going all night, bringing
bundles of screwed hay and other substitutes.
A west wind came also very kindly to their
assistance, carrying all the sounds of the workmen away from the town ; and the very moon
itself, then at full, while she gave them ample
light to work by, hung a hazy vail round the
hills, as if to screen them from too curious
observation. Washington stood through the
night hours among his faithful workmen, watch-
ing the ceaseless labor of their hands growing
into formidable defenses for American liberties

His heart was full of hope, hope that grew into joy, for he saw that every thing contributed to the success of his plans. Below him, under the full moon, lay the sleeping town, its sleeping soldiery, and its unsuspecting general, who might indeed have had his dreams broken by the incessant roar of cannon, but composed himself again to slumber, without a thought of danger for the morrow. While he took his last morning nap, the dawning day revealed to the astonished sentinels the frowning redoubts that crowned the brows of Dorchester Heights. Howe could scarcely believe that either his eyes or his glasses told the truth. He and his officers met in council. He told them that it must have been the work of at least twelve hundred men. His officers told him that 'it recalled the wonderful stories in Eastern romance of enchantment and the invisible agency of fairy hands.' The old sailor Admiral Shuldham, who commanded the squadron in the harbor, sent word to Howe that if they retained possession of the heights he could not keep a ship in the harbor. An assault or the evacuation was the alternative. The first was chosen. Lord Percy was to lead it, but the men remembered Bunker Hill and showed no enthusiasm. While they still debated, a violent storm set in and they could do nothing. It prevented them from landing troops from their boats, but did not prevent our New England farmers from toiling, and strengthening their works until Howe dared not attempt the assault. His mortification and that of his officers was unspeakable. ' One combination, concerted with faultless ability and suddenly executed, had in a few hours made their position untenable!'

" Nothing remained for them but to embark and sail away. But now the question was, Would Washington, whose artillery commanded the harbor, allow them to depart peaceably? General Howe humiliated himself to send proposals to Washington that he would leave the city unharmed provided Washington would suffer the fleet, with the troops, to sail out of the harbor unmolested. Washington accepted the bloodless victory. It was both a choice and a necessity with him at all times to spare his men and his powder, for of both he always had scant supply. A panic seized the British army. They precipated their leave-taking, and the citizens of Boston from every height, wharf, and hill for miles around, beheld with boundless joy the long procession of retreating sails. Coming into Boston, our army found that the British had left in their hasty flight two hundred and fifty pieces of cannon, many of their horses, and much forage and clothing. Better than all, for many days after, British ships were constantly arriving and entering the harbor, thinking to find their friends. These ships, with all their stores, among which were seven hundred barrels of powder, came into American hands. It was March 17, 1776. Who shall tell the joy of the Bostonians as their friends hurried in, and the pining exiles of poverty and want embraced those from whom they had been so long separated. For Washington what welcome and shouts of gratitude rent the air! The Selectmen of Boston addressed him thanks in due form, 'and the chief in reply paid a just tribute to their unparalleled fortitude.' 'A week later Washington attended the Thursday Lecture, which had been kept up since the days of Winthrop, and all rejoiced with exceeding ·joy at seeing this New England Zion once more a quiet habitation, a tabernacle that should never be taken down, of which not one of the stakes should ever be removed, nor one of the cords be broken ; and as the words were spoken it seemed as if the old century was holding out its hand to the new, and the Puritan ancestry of Massachusetts returned to bless the deliverer of their children !'

"Across the ocean, King George and Lord North sat moodily in council. The glory of the British arms was dimmed. The story of Lexington, Concord, Bunker Hill, and Boston ran over Europe like wild-fire. King Frederick of Prussia, the greatest military captain of his age, did not stint his courtly compliments of Washington and his army of militia; while at the court of France American valor was the theme of every tongue, and our heroes' names were familiar as household words. Affairs were going exactly to please the French king and his ministers, but they were not yet ready to say so openly. Secretly, however, vessels departed from French ports, laden with clothing and ammunition for the American army. The English people were in a state of ferment and open animosity against king and parliament; so much so that at one time it was to be feared that civil war would flame up in England on this American question.

"In the midst of this state of things parliament met. King George and his ministers stubbornly stood their ground. Agents again presented themselves with further petitions from Congress. Parliament refused to recognize an envoy from an American Congress. The king spurned petitions and petitioners. In vain the wisest statesmen of England raised their warning voice. Letters and petitions poured in from eminent individuals, corporations, and cities. In parliament Lord John Cavendish uttered these prophetic words : 'It is desired to send against them numerous armies and formidable fleets ; but they are at home surrounded by friends and abounding in all things. The English are at an immense distance, having for enemies climate, winds, seas, and armies. What wealth, what treasure will be necessary to subsist your troops in those distant countries ! Impenetrable forests, inaccessible mountains, will serve the Americans in case of disaster as so many retreats and fortresses, whence they will rush forth upon you anew. You will, therefore, be under a constant necessity to conquer or die, or, what is worse than death, to fly ignominiously to your ships. They will avail themselves of the knowledge of places which they only have to harass the British troops, intercept the ways, cut off supplies, surprise outposts, exhaust, consume, and prolong at will the war. *Imagine not that they will expose themselves to the hazard of battles.* They will vanquish us by fatigue, placed as we shall be at a distance of three thousand miles from our country. It will be easy for them, impossible for us, to receive continual reinforcements; the tardy succors that arrive to us by the Atlantic will not prevent our reverses; they will learn in our school the use of arms and the art of war, and they will eventually give their masters fatal proofs of their efficiency.' This prophecy was fulfilled to the letter.

" But wise counsels were lost on king and parliament; the enemies of America had the majority. One change, however, was observable : the Americans were no longer spoken of as cowards, but as wily and powerful foes. A large army was now to be raised and sent to subdue them. Where should it come from? In vain the recruiting officers raised the royal standard and beat their drums through the cities of England. The English people refused to enlist to fight for a bad cause and shed the blood of their friends and countrymen. What then ? They must go abroad and hire soldiers ; and King George went round knocking at the doors of the European kings begging for help.

" Did he, indeed, now?" said little Stevey, with a curious smile in his childish face.

" I don't mean that he went in person, Stevey," returned Aunt Edith, smiling, "he sent his servants in his name, but he does not figure less pitiably in history than if he had gone himself.

He wanted Russia to hire twenty thousand of her barbarous warriors ; but Queen Catharine declined to send her soldiers so far from home ; she might want them in the meantime. Then he applied to the United Provinces, but they refused. Holland returned for answer that it was beneath the dignity of a republic to meddle in the struggles of a foreign people for liberty. They had better success with the small German States, whose princes were generally in straits for money. They succeeded in employing here about eighteen thousand Hessians, who, together with twenty-five thousand English regulars, were dispatched as soon as possible to America. They enlisted some Scotch and Irish, and the recruiting officers were charged to enlist as many Canadians, Indians, and negroes as possible. They hoped by all these means to assemble an army of at least fifty thousand. They also passed a bill prohibiting all traffic with the thirteen colonies, so that no supplies of any kind should reach them from England. They declared that all American property, whether taken in vessels or on shore, should be the prizes of the officers and crews of the king's ships ; and all prisoners taken, no matter what their rank, should serve as common sailors on board English vessels. Lastly, no efforts were to be spared to break up the hated union of the colonies and to disperse the Congress. They knew if they could succeed in dividing the colonies by making mischief between them they could conquer them easily; but if they stood together in union they could not accomplish it.

"You may imagine the wrath and indignation which filled the land when this news was received from England. Hireling soldiery, Indian savages, negroes, and tories all coming against them! Meantime the captain of a British war-vessel had burned a town in Maine, named Falmouth, turning his guns upon it without warning, out of pure revenge. Lord Dunmore had also bombarded and burned Norfolk in Virginia, compelling its women and children to find shelter in the woods. Both these outrages were inexcusable, because they were not done during battle, as sometimes occurs without intention, but were deliberate acts of cruelty. More than all, Lord Dunmore used his efforts to promote insurrection among the African slaves. This fact was established beyond doubt, and the reason assigned for it was, that by this means the planters and farmers now in the army would be compelled to return to their homes for the defense of their wives and children. This was horrible; and all these things embittered the minds of the Americans against England. The fathers now saw that they could never live under English rule again. Washington gave his voice for independence. Lee, Henry, and Jefferson, of Virginia, all favored it. The Adamses and Franklin had long labored for it. The New England States, New York, and Virginia had all been witness to the horrors of war and the inhumanity of British officers and soldiers. As if a spur were wanting to urge forward the southern provinces to the same mind, it was applied just at this time.

"Dismayed at Yankee valor, the English determined to test Southern mettle, and we shall see how they found it. They hoped, because of the open, flat coast, to effect an easy landing and conquest of Carolina. The royal governor, who had not yet left his province, had assembled quite a force of tories. He had also written to the ministers of England, encouraging an attack on the coast of North Carolina, from which they could easily strike a blow, either at Virginia on the one hand or at South Carolina on the other. Accordingly, a fleet of eight war-vessels, well manned, with fifty transports, carrying General Clinton and an army of seven thousand men, were dispatched on this errand. The tories of North Carolina were ready at the place and time appointed ; not so the fleet and their English friends. They met unfriendly storms that beat them about backward when they would fain have gone forward, eastward instead of westward ; they arrived long after the appointed time to find that the tories, whom they expected would welcome and co-operate with them as guides and friends, had been attacked and dispersed by the patriots. Their first intention having thus been frustrated they resolved to attack Charleston, which was the hot-bed of treason in the South. The southern ' Sons of Liberty' gathered to its defense from every direction. Gadsden and Rutledge were there cheering on the people. Not a man but shouldered his gun or pick and spade. The slaves worked beside their masters and did faithful service. The chief sea-defense was a fort on Sullivan's Island, the command of which was given to a brave young officer named Moultrie, and for his successful defense of it the fort afterward received his name. The militia also had thrown up earthworks on shore to prevent the landing of the army to co-operate with the fleet. Having done all, they stood to their arms and waited for the attack. The plan of the British general was a good one. The ships were to cannonade Fort Moultrie in front while the army was to land on the island in the rear, thus cutting off the retreat of the garrison. The fort taken, they were to attack and capture the city. The two largest frigates, however, in passing the bar, to get a favorable position to open fire, struck, so that the crews were obliged to throw over part of their guns to lighten them off. At last, all being in position, five vessels, having one hundred and eighty-six guns in all, opened fire upon the gallant Moultrie and his little band, who had only one tenth as many guns, and so little powder that he was obliged to economize his firing and repress the ardor of his men."

"O, I'm so tired of hearing that they never had powder enough," said Harry, with vexation in his face.

"I am tired of telling it too, but it was so— they never did have enough. You must remember our fathers had been for years cultivating the arts of peace. They were not a military people, and were not ready for this war. Well, they fired slowly, but with great precision and with telling effect. So great was the disparity of force that the British thought two broadsides would end the struggle, and they had come up very near the fort ; but they did not take 'palmetto' into their account. Fort Moultrie looked

a frail, rude affair, but it was built of soft, fibrous,
spongy palmetto logs, in which the balls found
a lodgment without splintering or penetrating.
The fort trembled and creaked, and even groaned
a little, but that was all."

"Is it time for us to call for three groans?"
said Harry.

"Not quite yet, Harry. The American gunners had poured a murderous fire into the
English ships, especially complimenting the
flag-ship of fifty guns, with the British admiral,
Sir Peter Parker, and the royal governor of
South Carolina aboard. They swept the deck,
so that at one time the commodore stood there
alone. Morris, his captain, was carried off
wounded, and, after suffering amputation of an
arm, insisted upon returning on deck and as-
suming command. But another ball gave him
his death-wound."

"He was a brave Englishman," said Albert,
"and died at his post."

"He was, indeed; let us give him honor.
They fought bravely—no blame can be attached
to the navy—and their eyes looked anxiously,
but vainly, for the landing of the army to divert
from them the fire of the fort. Having rashly
taken position so near, they could not now
retire, as both wind and tide had left them.

Several of the vessels, for the time disabled, swung round into positions most favorable for the execution of the American gunners.

"But Moultrie's fire now slackened and finally ceased. Their ammunition was gone, and Sir Peter Parker still hoped, if the army would but carry out their part of the programme, that they could yet effect the capture of the fort and city. He had dispatched three of his vessels to cover their landing, but, unfortunately for them, their pilots were at fault ; they ran hopelessly aground on the sand-bars, and were of no more use than if they had been laid up high and dry in English docks."

"Ah! Charleston harbor is a troublesome place," chuckled Harry. "Now you *are* there and now you're *not* there. I wonder how they liked Southern mettle by this time. Hurra for our side!"

"Hush, Harry," said Nannie, "you're such a rowdy, interrupting the story."

"Let him effervesce," said Aunt Edith. "It will come out in stump oratory some of these days. To continue, Clinton, the British general, did put his men into small boats, but upon approaching the landing he found it so vigilantly guarded that he ordered his men back to their positions. Meantime the citizens of Charleston watched from their house-tops and wharves of the city, while the sea-breezes brought the noise and hot breath of battle into their very faces. They watched and wished, and some of them prayed ; they were the sons and grandsons of the old Huguenot stock, who loved their civil and religious liberties more than their lives. It was the same spirit that had animated the men of Lexington and Concord a year before. The brave Christopher Gadsden was in command at Fort Johnson, within hearing, and many a cheer came over the blue waters from his regiment to their brothers of Moultrie, begrimed with the sweat and smoke of battle. About this time their flag was shot away and fell over the ramparts. Sergeant Jasper cried out to Moultrie, ' Colonel, don't let us fight without a flag ! '

"' What can you do ?' asked Moultrie ; ' the staff is broken.'

"' Then,' said Jasper, ' I'll fix it on a halberd and place it on the merlon of the bastion next the enemy ;' and, leaping through an embrasure and braving the thickest of the enemy's fire, he took up the flag, returned with it safely, and planted it where he had promised. Another brave fellow fell mortally wounded and exclaimed, ' I am dying ; but, comrades, don't

13

let the cause of liberty expire with me this day.'
Let their names be linked with those of Jonas
Parker and Isaac Davis, of Lexington Green
and Concord Bridge.   They were brothers.

" When the people of Charleston heard Moultrie's fire slacken and then cease, their hearts
trembled with fear ; but he sent a messenger
up to the city to ask for more powder and to
say, ' All's well.'   Rutledge sent him three hundred pounds of powder, with the words, ' Honor
and victory to you and our worthy countrymen
with you.   Do not make too free with your
cannon.   Be cool and do mischief.'   At five
o'clock in the evening Moultrie again ordered
the men to their guns.   The British began to
show signs of weariness.   The sun went down
and left the battle still raging.   About nine
o'clock, after a cannonade of ten hours, his
crews worn down, his vessels much disabled,
having given up all hope of help from the land
forces, ' Sir Peter slipped his cable and dropped
down with the tide.'   The Americans lost eleven
killed and twenty-six wounded.   The British
fleet lost two hundred in killed and wounded.
They managed to get off all their vessels, in a
mangled state, except the ' Acteon,' one of the
three on the sand-bar.   The crew set her on fire
and left her.   Some brave fellows from the fort

boarded her while burning, turned her guns upon the retiring vessels, and loaded three boats from her stores. 'A half hour after they left her she blew up, and, to the eyes of the Carolinians, the pillar of smoke as it rose from the vessel took the form of the palmetto.' So crippled were the British vessels that it was weeks before they could get away from the Southern waters."

"And what did they say of Southern mettle?" asked Nannie.

"That it had as true ring as Yankee valor. This was a most important victory. Three years passed before the British ventured again on Southern soil. This attack on Charleston had diverted the tide of battle from the North for some months, and gave Washington time to prepare for the threatened attack on New York. This naval battle was fought on the 28th of June, 1776. Swift couriers carried the news to the Congress at Philadelphia, and spurred on the halting spirits for 'Independence.' In England the failure of this attack on Charleston caused intense regret and sorrow. They had been led to believe that the tories, the king's friends, were largely in the majority in the South, and that the capture of Charleston meant the subjugation of the Carolinas. They were now undeceived."

CHAPTER XIV.

A Nation is Born in a Day—July 4, 1776—Salutatory—
Declaration of Independence—Thomas Jefferson—
England Hurls all her Military Resources upon
Washington's Army—New York Lost, but the
Cause Saved.

" AND what did they say in Philadelphia to the heroes of Fort Moultrie?" asked Nannie.

"They voted them thanks, and a sword to Sergeant Jasper; and Moultrie shone like the morning star, as the dawn of American Independence struggled into perfect day. The hours were heavy with human hopes and destinies as those great spirits argued out the necessity and wisdom of declaring America a free and independent nation. Lee and Henry, the Adamses and Franklin, gave all their eloquence in favor of independence. The people were calling for it all over the land, urging their delegates on. Thomas Jefferson, the great Virginian, just thirty-three years old, as he listened to the voice of the American people rolling up, wave on wave, like the voice of many waters, heard it as the voice of God. He seized the nation's inspiration, and married it to the match-

less music of the Declaration of Independence.
It was Young America then, and now that we
have grown older we still remember the dreams
of our youth. When they heard the burning

JEFFERSON.

words the Fathers pronounced it very good,
and every-where the people shouted for joy
and said, 'Yes, that is it; that is what we felt,
and this man has spoken it for us. And the
Fathers launched this good ship of State on
the waters of time, and the Scripture was ful-

filled which says, 'A nation shall be born in a day.'

"Children," continued Aunt. Edith, in a quicker tone of voice, "we sit here to-night and repeat this story as if it were only a thing of beauty, lightly, gracefully, and easily accomplished. But there is another side to the story. The nation was now beyond dispute a nation of traitors. They had thrown off all allegiance to King George and England. In the colonies the royal governors had been set aside; most of them had returned to England, as they had no power to enforce their own authority. The governments of the different colonies were pure democracies, their assemblies being elected and authorized immediately from the people, without reference to charters or king's seal. Their delegates to Congress were called the ringleaders of treason, a price would be set upon their heads, and if taken their lives would be the forfeit of their political crimes. As the Fathers gathered round to sign their names to the Declaration of Independence, 'pledging their lives, fortunes, and sacred honor' to maintain and defend it, one of them said, 'We must stand by each other and hang together in this matter;' and Franklin wittily added, 'Yes, certainly, otherwise we shall all hang separately.'

" We are to keep in mind that England was
the most powerful nation in the world. She
was mistress on the ocean ; her army and navy
were fully armed and equipped. She had vast
resources, and had now determined to put forth
all her power to crush us. It seemed like madness for America to undertake to withstand her.
In some respects our country was poor ; though
there was abundance of provisions, there was
very little gold or silver. War is a very expensive business. Clothing and arms must be
bought in Europe, and paid for in gold and
silver, for American paper money was worth
nothing out of the country. The bills of credit
that Congress issued had not much credit with
our own people, because they might never be
able to make them good. Congress, though it
represented the American government, was not
sufficiently strong and responsible to establish
the financial credit of the nation. Its power
rested only on the good-will of the people ; it
was the early and feeble beginning of the great,
wise, and strong government that was afterward established by the Fathers, that to-day
protects and governs us. Though they had
great hope and faith in Congress, yet the people
felt that they had entered upon an experiment.
There were fears along with the hopes, while

many felt strong doubts whether the authority of Congress could hold the country firmly together amid the shocks of war. So the Fathers could only feel their way along carefully and slowly, step by step, not doing always the best and wisest things, but being obliged often to do the next best. One of the greatest of their mistakes was that they did not heed Washington's advice. He urged them to raise a large army at once, and to enlist their soldiers for the entire war. Congress failed to do this because the people were prejudiced against large standing armies. They knew that was the way the people of European countries were held down under the will of kings or privileged classes, and they feared lest some ambitious man should contrive to put himself at the head of the army, seize the reins of power, and drive the country into a worse despotism than that from which they had escaped. This has often been done ; history is full of these examples. They enlisted their soldiers for six months or a year. The consequence was Washington's difficulties were increased a hundredfold and much of his labor thrown away. Scarcely had he equipped and drilled the raw militia when they melted away before his eyes, their term being expired. They were always coming and going out of his camp.

He protested again and again, but Congress failed to comply. Public sentiment was against it, and they hoped the war would not last over a year. Amid the exultations of the people and the rejoicings of Congress over the Declaration of Independence came a courier from Washington, in his camp at New York, announcing that the British fleet and army were in the harbor. 'I am hopeful,' wrote the general, 'that we shall get some reinforcements before they are prepared to attack; be that as it may, I shall make the best disposition I can of our troops.' While some quailed before the prospect, he moved serenely among his soldiers, strengthening and encouraging them for the coming conflict. The eloquent words of the Declaration of Independence had been pronounced; but it remained for Washington and his men to make it good with trusty swords and cannon balls. Congress had weakened his army by ordering him to send several regiments to Canada, against not only his judgment, but his warm expostulations. He obeyed the order, and then made every effort to rectify the mischief of such a mistake.

"It being now clear that the object of the British was the capture of the city of New York, Washington ordered every available man that could be spared from other points to join his camp. Thus reinforced his army numbered about twenty-five thousand. Not more than one half were armed or fit for service, some never having seen the smoke of battle before; very different from the army about to land and attack them. The whole land and naval force under the brothers General and Admiral Howe and General Clinton, together with the Hessians, under very able generals, would reach thirty-five thousand of the best troops Europe could boast; men trained to arms; men who had actually lived in battle. They were English regulars, full of British pride, sorely wounded at having lost their reputation for the first time in a wrestle with these despised American farmers, hunters, and country gentlemen. There was also the greatest emulation between the English and Germans, both soldiers and officers. It was a humiliation to the English that it had been found necessary to call the Germans to their help, while the Germans were equally determined not to be eclipsed by English valor. As to equipments, nothing was wanting that the military magazines of Europe could supply; they were armed to the teeth.

"Washington knew all this, and as he looked at the hastily gathered multitude of men in his camp, badly clothed, unarmed, and undisciplined, though brave and willing, he knew that by all human calculations it was madness to bring the two together in battle ; the raw militia must go down before the heavy English and German battalions. Fear, it may be, he felt, but not despair. He had given himself to this cause, to live and to die for it and in it. He busied himself with all the energy of his nature to use every man and every musket to the best advantage, with a serene faith that God, who has given his word always to protect the just cause, would himself enter the arena and get his own victory. He whom 'winds and seas obey,' who 'plants his footsteps in the sea and rides upon the storm,' had already interfered in their favor. Let me explain how. The British forces were sent in three divisions. The first, under Sir Peter Parker by sea and General Clinton by land, was to operate in the South. The second division, under General Howe by land and Admiral Howe by sea, was to capture New York. The admiral with his ships would hold the harbor and command the city, while the general would ascend the Hudson River to Albany. Still another division, under General Carleton of Canada, was to descend by Lakes Champlain and George, retaking the Forts Ti-

conderoga and Crown Point, and join Howe at
Albany. Thus the New England colonies would
be entirely separated from the Middle colonies.
Pressed on all sides at the same time—for these
operations were to go on simultaneously—it
would be impossible for the Americans to oppose a sufficient force at all these points, and
the rebellion would be speedily crushed. The
plan was admirable. But you have seen how
the expedition to the South failed, by reason of
contrary winds bringing them out of time, to
encounter a far more spirited resistance than
they expected. We shall see as we proceed
how it fared with the rest of this great military
plan. ·General Clinton, after idly looking on,
while Moultrie splintered up Sir Peter Parker's
vessels, sailed away to join General Howe in
New York Harbor. Admiral Lord Howe, on
leaving England, had been instructed to offer,
upon his arrival here, peaceful overtures and
pardon to all who should lay down their arms
and return to their allegiance to the king ; for
the British authorities were somewhat startled
by the bold position Congress assumed. Before offering battle, therefore, he sent a letter to
the general-in-chief, directed simply to George
Washington, Esq. The general declined to receive it, as it did not express his public rank

and office, and as a private individual he could
not hold any communication with the king's
officers. Lord Howe did not wish to let a mere
matter of ceremonial prevent the interview,
neither did he wish to acknowledge the commander-in-chief of the rebel nation officially.
He sent a second letter, addressed to George
Washington, etc., etc., etc., etc. An adjutant-
general was sent to present it in person. On
being introduced into Washington's presence
he addressed him with the title of ' Excellency.'
Washington received him with great politeness,
but, with greater dignity, declining still to receive or read the letter. You see, dear children,
it was not merely a point of ceremony that he
contended for. Since July Fourth, America had
set forth her claims as a free and independent
nation. Washington was now commander-in-
chief of the national army, nor would he bate
one jot or tittle, of his rank and office. In refusing to recognize him, they refused to recognize
the nation. Washington explained to the bearer
of the letter, ' that a letter written to a person
invested with a public character should specify
it, otherwise it could not be distinguished from
a private letter. That it was true *et ceteras*
implied every thing, but it was no less true
that they implied nothing, and that he could

receive no letter on public affairs that did not designate his rank and office.' Congress much applauded this conduct of Washington, and ordered all officers to make it the rule of their conduct.

"Nothing remained but to come to battle. Had Washington reasoned and acted only as a soldier, he would doubtless not have accepted an open field fight; but he reflected that by falling back before the enemy he would uncover the weakness of his army. Also, to yield New York without a blow would expose them to the charge of cowardice, which would rejoice the foe and dispirit the Americans. Likewise, it was exceedingly important to retain the city if possible. Howe landed his troops without opposition on Long Island, not far from where Brooklyn now stands. All preparations being completed, the attack was made on the American lines. Heavy masses of German and English troops were hurled against Washington's raw militia. They fought well for a time, but Washington beheld from the Heights of Brooklyn what he feared would come to pass, the American ranks broken, scattered, and flying in confusion. He saw a brave band of Marylanders, the sons of the best men in the province, surrounded and absolutely cut to pieces.

The general uttered an exclamation of anguish at the sight. Night closed on the bloody field. Three thousand were killed, wounded, and prisoners. The British loss was not so great ; they had fresh forces to bring into the field, and fully intended to renew the battle on the next day. Washington did not. It stormed for two days and nights so that nothing could be done on either side. On the third night Washington passed all his army baggage, artillery, and entire effects across the East River into New York. Providence seemed to watch over them ; though 'cast down' they were not to be 'destroyed.' About two o'clock in the morning a thick fog, unusual at that season, covered Long Island, while the air was perfectly clear on the New York side. It was July 29, 1776. When the sun drank up the fog the British general saw with vexation that the American army had literally slipped through his fingers. Military critics called this safe retreat, under the very eye of a powerful and victorious enemy, a prodigy of skill and wisdom.

" The effects of the defeat upon the spirit of the American army was most disastrous. Up to this time they had imagined that courage would accomplish every thing. Now that it had yielded before the heavy ranks and superior equipments of European discipline they sunk into despondency, and concluded it could do nothing. This was wrong. They at first overrated themselves ; now they underrated themselves. And, notwithstanding Washington's exhortations and persuasions, they deserted by whole companies. The New England militia, who had only enlisted for a few weeks to assist in the defense of New York, insisted upon returning at the end of the time to be ready for home defense, for the British had now hundreds of vessels in our waters, and the whole New England coast lay open to their wrath.

"In this state of things, with the British vessels in the East River, and General Howe preparing to cross with his army in pursuit, Washington called a council of his officers, and the decision was to abandon New York. Washington's first care now was to preserve the remains of his army, and this could only be done by avoiding another battle. General Howe's object was to force the general to battle by hot pursuit of him. Washington therefore retired to a place called Kingsbridge, a few miles above New York, and there intrenched himself. Leaving a garrison in the city, General Howe pushed on after him. Finding his positions rather formidable he hesitated to attack, and encamped in the neighborhood, pondering what next.

"During this time, the armies lying close to each other, many little skirmishes occurred in which the Americans got much the better of their enemies, and so plucked up courage once more. This was just what Washington wished. To win back their confidence in themselves would be worth more than to win a battle. They began to lose some of their terror of their new enemies, the Hessians, which had been extreme. Children, I want you to notice now that Washington's movements were all on the defensive, from the necessity of the case. He was so much weaker in every way than his enemy that his highest aim was to make the best of a very bad case. This whole campaign was an effort, not to gain any thing, but to prevent the utter failure of the American cause. Albert, what does campaign mean ?"

"It means a number of battles and military movements, I think."

"Yes, for the accomplishment of some certain object. This campaign of Howe's began with his landing on Long Island in July, and lasted up to the new year. It was a rare game of chess between the two generals, played with

14

marked ability by both, though with great disadvantage on Washington's side. He had no plan of his own, and could have none. His only care was to study Howe's movements, penetrate his designs, **and then** disappoint and thwart him."

CHAPTER XV.

Washington Retreats through New Jersey—Disaster "Follows Fast and Follows Faster"—Washington's Faith and Courage—He Attempts the Impossible and Accomplishes It—Recrosses the Delaware, Saves Philadelphia, and Chases the British Back to New York.

"WHERE did we leave Washington last evening?" asked Aunt Edith of her little group of listeners.

"Encamped at Kingsbridge," answered several voices.

"Correct. Washington, from certain movements of Howe, guessed the conclusion he had come to—not to attack him at Kingsbridge, as it would cost him too many lives to dislodge the Americans, but, instead, to get in his rear, and take a higher position at White Plains. That would be to flank Washington's army, which no good general will ever allow if he can help it. Therefore Washington chose himself to occupy that position; broke up his camp and marched away at night, and Howe found himself again outgeneraled. He followed at once and brought on a battle in which neither side could claim a victory, and Washington again moved with his army still higher up into a rough, difficult hill country, where Howe, finding it impossible either to dislodge him, or coax or force him to a fight, turned back and addressed himself to the capture of Forts Washington and Lee, the northern river defenses of New York, a few miles above the city. Washington wrote advising their evacuation, though not commanding it. Colonel Magraw at Fort Washington with a large garrison was sanguine of holding it. The assault was made with great vigor, principally by the Germans, who lost a thousand men in taking the outer defenses. After a brave defense, Colonel Magraw was compelled to surrender. Between two and three thousand troops fell prisoners into British hands, and at this critical time were lost to their country's service. Washington deplored this calamity, and at once ordered the evacuation of Fort Lee, on the opposite bank of the Hudson. He crossed the river himself, and marched down its western bank in order to bring the scattered forces together. Emboldened by success, Howe had ordered a force to cross the Hudson and invest Fort Lee, which contained a garrison of two thousand men. So rapid were his movements that the garrison had barely time to escape, leaving all their artillery, baggage, provisions, and, worst of all, their tents, which they now greatly needed, for November winds were scattering the last leaves from the trees."

"O dear! O dear!" moaned little Stevey.

"That was close quarters, indeed," said Harry.

"Please tell us, aunty," said Nannie, anxiously, "What did Washington do?"

"What did Washington do? He moved about grandly; showed himself among his dejected soldiers serene, calm, and patient; and a light shone in his eyes that told of 'hoping against hope.' He gathered all the scattered forces together and prepared to retreat into New Jersey. Take courage, Stevey, (looking into the little boy's anxious eyes,) 'all's not lost that's in danger.' Do you remember what was the programme for the armies of New York and Canada, Albert?"

"Yes, aunty. You said Carleton was to come down the lakes to Albany, and Howe was to go up the Hudson River, and thus holding the river and lakes, they would divide New England from the rest of the colonies."

"Very well. Now notice, that Washington's skillful maneuvering had occupied Howe in the vicinity of New York until so late in the season that that plan failed utterly. Carleton had executed his part of it, coming down the lakes and under the very walls of Ticonderoga, which was too strongly fortified and garrisoned for him to assault without Howe's co-operation. Hearing nothing from Howe, except that he had gone to New Jersey, he found himself at the beginning of winter far from home, in an enemy's country, without provisions for his army. He was obliged, therefore, to conduct his army back into Canada, and wait until next year to complete his work.

"Howe dared not venture too far from New York while Washington continued in its vicinity with his army, for he still kept up a show of an army, and kept his standard flying. Howe always gave him credit for a much larger army than he really had, and Washington took very good care not to let him get near enough to count his men. Howe consoled himself for the failure of his Hudson River plan with the prospect of a still greater prize—nothing less than the city of Philadelphia itself. He fancied that Washington's dispirited and defeated army would be unable to resist him further; he should capture the city, the capital of the so-called confederacy, disperse the Congress, receive the submission of the colonies, and thus have the glory of ending the war himself. Washington soon discovered what Howe meant to do. He now called all the troops that could be spared from the lake defenses, and ordered the New Jersey and Pennsylvania militia to assemble near Philadelphia. He fell slowly back, skirmishing, and delaying the advance of the British army as long as possible, to gain time for his reinforcements to arrive. The British followed, spreading themselves well over the eastern part of New Jersey; their soldiers committing all sorts of excesses and cruelties, burning and plundering, especially the rude German barbarians, until the very name of Hessian became a terror to American ears. It wrung the heart of Washington to know what these poor people suffered, and he unable to shield them from it. He continued to fall back, and finally passed the Delaware, destroying the bridges, and drawing the boats after him to the other side.

"Howe, arriving upon its east bank, found a wide and rapid river between him and Washington, with the bridges gone. There was a risk in trusting himself on the other side, thus putting the river between him and his magazines, which were in Princeton and Brunswick; for he was compelled to drag his provisions after him. It was mid-winter now, and he was in the country of an enemy who refused to feed

him ; and even the tories dared not do it, except by stealth. He therefore distributed his
army in small divisions among the towns on the
east side of the river, and waited for Jack Frost
to build him an ice-bridge over which he could
lead his army into Philadelphia.

"Washington saw these movements with delight. Though his army, by disease and deser-
tions, had fallen away to a mere skeleton, yet
those who remained were a faithful and a valiant
few, and he did not despair yet, by some rapid,
unexpected movement, to give a favorable turn
to affairs. It was Christmas night. The Hessians had finished their revels, and had gone to
sleep toward the small morning hours. Washington had planned three several attacks. His
own division was to cross the Delaware at
Trenton, where Colonel Rahl was encamped
·with a body of German troops. There was a
high wind, a rapid current, a driving snow-
storm, and the river full of floating blocks of
ice. Howe and his officers as soon expected
an enemy to drop out of the clouds as for one to
attempt the passage of the river under such circumstances. But it was just some such superhuman achievement that was needed at this
time, and Washington resolved to do it. Only
the division which he commanded in person

Washington Crossing the Delaware.

96 10.

succeeded in passing the river. Both the others were blocked in the ice, and with great peril extricated themselves and returned to the camp.

"Washington had hoped to effect a landing at midnight, but the ice and biting cold delayed them, and it was gray dawn before all were landed. What a night they had spent, wrestling with the elements! What surging waves of hope and fear had beat about that great man's heart! They attacked immediately. Colonel Rahl attempted to form for battle, but the surprise and impetuosity of the attack, for the general-in-chief seemed to impart to every one of his soldiers a portion of his own spirit, threw them into hopeless confusion. They would have gladly escaped by flight, but Washington had posted his men so as to cut off retreat. Colonel Rahl fell mortally wounded, and the Hessians struck their colors. Only ten Americans were killed and wounded. Of the Hessians Colonel Rahl, six officers, and forty men were killed, and over a thousand, with their arms, cannon, and baggage, were made prisoners, and safely conveyed across the Delaware, marched to Philadelphia, and paraded through the city.

"This victory was most timely. The army was filled with enthusiasm, and Washington determined at once, mid-winter as it was, to assume the offensive. He led his army back over the Delaware ; a panic seized the British, and they retreated toward Brunswick, fearing for the safety of their magazines gathered there. Washington followed, haunting the hills of New Jersey with his phantom army ; hovering round the homesteads and villages to protect the terrified women and children from the brutal soldiery ; sweeping down upon the enemy's foraging parties like fitful winter gusts, capturing or dispersing them, and compelling them to keep within their lines ; appearing where least expected, and disappearing when most wanted to remain. If assailed by large numbers, Washington led his hungry, frost-bitten, half-naked heroes up into some rocky fastness for safety and refreshment ; if followed there, creeping stealthily away like the mountain mists, to appear again in some unexpected quarter. In vain did Howe maneuver to bring him to battle. Yet with an army twenty thousand strong, while Washington had never more than three thousand, the British general dared not march again toward Philadelphia.

" The campaign for 1776 was ended, and the plans of the British ministry, sustained as they were by overwhelming forces, had failed every-where. Now, dear children, if you will look very attentively with your sharp young eyes at this chapter of history, you will see defeat crowned with the fruits of victory, and victory slink away at the last, dragging defeat at its heels. The praying people, those who believe in God and know that he rules in the armies of men, said, 'It is the Lord's doings, and marvelous in our eyes.' The superhuman wisdom of Washington, in achieving such results with means so inadequate, brought him great glory. His name was every-where spoken with reverence. The most distinguished writers and illustrious persons in Europe lavished upon him, with pen and tongue, praises and congratulations. Meantime Congress had drawn up ' Articles of Confederation for the thirteen United States,' and had appointed ministers to represent the new nation at the courts of Europe, to induce them to acknowledge them and treat with them in their new character. Hoping more from France than from any other nation, they sent to that country Benjamin Franklin. His name and his fame had long preceded him at the French court. Though the snows of winter crowned his venerable head, for he had passed his threescore and ten years, yet the fire of his genius was not dim by reason of his age. His wit was as keen as at twenty, and his vivacity still undiminished. He was the object of universal admiration and curiosity, the people thronged his steps when he appeared in public, and no foreigner had ever such homage at the French court, where wit and philosophy always receive attention. His mission was to induce the King of France openly to espouse the cause of America and recognize her as a nation. This was a grave matter ; it meant to go to war with England ; that is, it would be such an insult to England for France to acknowledge her rebel colonies as a nation that England would be compelled in . honor to declare war against France.

"France held back for several good reasons. She was not exactly ready, though she was get-- ting ready with all speed, building formidable war vessels and strengthening both army and navy. Moreover, she wanted to be satisfied that the American people were not only fully determined to cut loose from England forever, but she also waited to see whether they would show the ability to defend themselves against the mighty armies and fleets that England had sent against them. Though the French declined to openly declare themselves, yet they continued to give every secret assistance possible, loaning the Americans money, selling them arms and

clothing, with promises to come openly to their
aid at no distant day. Now I want to explain
to you, children, that the French court, king and
ministers, had no real sympathy with our Fathers in their struggles to establish a republican
form of government. Kings and the supporters
of kings are the natural enemies of republics.
The secret of their good wishes for the American rebellion was that they hated England, and
wanted to see her power reduced by the loss of
her colonies. If America became an independent nation she would trade with France as freely
as she had formerly with England, which would
make France rich as she had made England.
The same reasons influenced Spain also, and the
other European nations, for they all bore an
envy, if not a hatred, to England, and had some
act of wrong or tyranny to avenge. The proba-
bility was that if France embraced the cause
of America, so also would Spain and Holland,
and thus a general European war would blaze
up. Our Fathers foresaw this, so also did wise
men in England. The great Chatham warned
the king and the ministers of it, but they would
not heed it. Noble spirits in every nation sym-
pathized with the infant republic ; the heroic resistance of the Americans excited the most intense interest and admiration among brave and

generous natures every-where. They showed their sympathy, not only in words of cheer, but they left home and friends and country, some of them at their own expense, to come to America. Men of rank and fortune presented themselves before the great American chief, feeling a high honor to serve such a cause under such a leader. The gallant young Frenchman, the Marquis de La Fayette, at the age of twenty-two, left his native land, a home of luxury, and his young wife, so strongly was he drawn to the cause of liberty and the character and person of Washington, whom he loved with an affection passing the love of women."

CHAPTER XVI.

Ticonderoga Surrenders to Burgoyne—Joy in England—Sorrow in America—The Tide Turns—Burgoyne Surrenders his Whole Army to Gen. Gates —Joy in America—Sorrow in England.

" THIS evening, children, we will go up among the lakes of New York and see what was passing there. It was now the spring of 1777, and the British were preparing for a summer campaign. The plan of warfare that had been attempted the year before was not altered, for the British ministers still thought it the best that could be devised. But they dispatched Burgoyne to the command of the Canadian army, for General Carleton had failed to give satisfaction there. They thought he had not shown sufficient vigor in his war measures. He hesitated to employ Indians, not only because of their barbarity, but because of the difficulty of bringing them under military discipline. In this he showed good generalship, as we shall hereafter see. His kindness and humanity to his American prisoners were also condemned. Let us remember it to his honor. He treated his prisoners with all the kindness the laws of war allowed, had the sick carefully nursed, and, pitying the sufferings of our poor half-naked soldiers amid the rigors of a Canadian winter, he clothed them and sent them home, only requiring them to take oath not to fight again against his Majesty King George the Third. We take leave of him with regret.

" Burgoyne was a very ambitious man and a great boaster. He made large promises of what he could do, and the British ministers gave him rank over Gen. Carleton, who soon after asked leave to resign. Burgoyne, upon arriving in Canada, dispatched agents to the Indian tribes to gather a large force of Indians, enlisted as many Canadians as possible, and with an army of ten thousand, consisting of British, Germans, Canadians, and Indians, proceeded down the lakes to reduce Fort Ticonderoga. He issued proclamations to the people promising pardon to all who would join him, or would take oath not to aid in any manner the revolutionary party ; also threatening all who resisted the authority of the British government with utter destruction. He reminded them of his Indian allies, who would scent them out if they attempted to conceal themselves to escape his wrath. This bloody proclamation covered his name with infamy, and instead of making the people fear him, only made them hate him and the king who had sent him to terrify an innocent people.

" They knew if the Indians were turned upon them they would have no mercy in any case, for they murdered and plundered friends and foes, asking no questions. The whole country flew to arms to join General Schuyler at Fort Edward. You see Forts St. John, Chambly, and Crown Point—show them to the children, Albert.

" These had all fallen into General Carleton's possession the summer before, and Burgoyne now proceeded to capture, destroy, or drive before him the American vessels on the lakes. In due time he arrived under the walls of Ticonderoga, the last and strongest of all the lake defenses. It had been armed and garrisoned as strongly as the military stores of the Americans would allow. General St. Clair defended it, and the people never thought it possible that it could be taken either by siege or assault. But there was one negligence of which the Americans were guilty. In the vicinity of the fort rises a steep, difficult eminence called Mount Defiance. It commands the fort. The

15

Americans took counsel concerning it. They could illy spare the artillery from their works to fortify it, and they rested in the hope that the difficulty and labor of the work would prevent the British from attempting to drag their artillery to its summit. They reckoned amiss. Burgoyne's army was splendidly equipped with abundance of the heaviest artillery. He comprehended the importance of the operation, and ordered it to be done. In a week of great toil and labor it was accomplished, and the next best thing for St. Clair to do was to evacuate the fort and escape with the garrison to Fort Edward, below, where Schuyler was gathering his army. Unfortunately, St. Clair's garrison had delayed too long to make a wise or well-ordered retreat. They were discovered, and pursued both by land and water. * They were obliged to blow up their shipping, and so hot was the pursuit that they were forced to abandon their batteaux, containing baggage, stores, and arms, which all fell into British hands. Those by land were pursued and scattered, and many perished of hunger in the woods ; but few were able to join Schuyler. When all the fugitives arrived, after their perils by water and in the wilderness, by the sword of their enemies and the scalping knife of the savages, Schuy-

ler could count only about four thousand dispirited troops to oppose to Burgoyne's army,
flushed with victory, and armed and equipped
beyond what was necessary.

" The news of the fall of this powerful fortress,
together with the loss of one hundred and twen-
ty-eight pieces of artillery, baggage, arms, and
immense quantities of stores and provisions, fell
like a sound of doom over the land. The news
was dispatched immediately to England, and
was received there with unbounded joy. Together with the details of what had already been
done, Burgoyne was profuse of his boasts of
certain victory to crown his future movements.
The Ministry were intoxicated with joy. They
strutted about the court prophesying the speedy
termination of the war and the submission
of the colonies."

" Yes," said Nannie, in a tone of vexation,
" I can almost hear their very words. 'There,
didn't I tell you so ? You wouldn't mind me ;
I knew it would turn out this way.' It always
tries my temper to hear people say, ' There, I
told you so ! ' I run right out of hearing."

" Well, the friends of America were obliged to
hear a great deal of this kind of talk, and indeed
they had nothing to answer, and were quite put
to silence."

"I hope the Fathers didn't lose heart, I am sure Washington didn't," continued the little girl, trying to prop up her own courage.

"O no! they felt the greatness of the calamity, and Washington hurried forward all the men he could possibly spare, sent General Gates to take command, and sent with him Arnold and Morgan. Congress dispatched agents to Europe to put the best face possible on affairs, especially at the French court.

Burgoyne, in the meantime, having left a garrison at Ticonderoga, pursued the Americans down Wood Creek, took Fort Skeenesborough, and, lower down, Fort Anne. He had now a wilderness to penetrate to arrive at Fort Edward, where Schuyler was. Burgoyne's provisions, magazines, and hospitals were now far in his rear, at Crown Point and Ticonderoga, and it was becoming very troublesome to keep his army supplied. The aspect of things began to change. General Schuyler had, very wisely, ordered all provisions to be secreted or removed, and the cattle to be driven back to remote parts of the country. The British army began to be pinched with hunger. It was yet a long distance to Albany, where Burgoyne was to meet General Howe. He was in a wilderness that could furnish no supplies for his army, and the people

were thoroughly unfriendly. He found out that
the Americans had large magazines of provisions at Bennington, in Vermont, and he sent
quite a detachment of troops there to seize them,
but the Vermont militia heard of their intended
visit. They met them quite unexpectedly, indeed laid in wait for them, and, after a sharp
battle, dispersed and pursued them, killing or
capturing a large number. His Indian allies,
too, gave Burgoyne a great deal of trouble.
They were very disobedient and unmanage-
able. All this helped to disorganize his own
troops. They came and went at pleasure, and
the officers secretly feared lest they should
turn their arms upon their friends. Courier
after courier was dispatched to Albany to learn
something of Howe's movements, but no light
came from that quarter. Howe had General
Washington to look after and New York to
keep. Burgoyne determined to push on through
the wilderness to Fort Edward : the march was
full of toil and danger. He rebuilt forty bridges
that Schuyler had destroyed in his retreat.
The Americans had also blocked up the roads
behind them by felling huge forest trees. This
made it very difficult for the British to travel,
especially as they were compelled to drag their
provisions all the way with them.

"Burgoyne could not endure the thought of his brilliant military exploits coming at last to grief. He hoped to be able to get out of the woods and reach Albany, where he could be provisioned by Howe. His case became critical. Having failed to obtain provisions at Bennington, he sent a force into the country of the Mohawk Indians; but Arnold had gone there, and, encountering the British troops, had dispersed and driven them back to the lakes, where they floated down and joined the main army. Upon arriving at Fort Edward they found that Schuyler had dismantled that fort and retreated to Stillwater, where Gates had assumed command.

"Every day the prospects of the Americans grew brighter. Their recent successes had raised their spirits. It was now August; the harvests were gathered, and the militia, farmers, and, in short, every body, seized their guns and hastened to Schuyler's camp. All this time Burgoyne was getting further and further from his magazines; indeed, it was no longer possible to bring his provisions, for the militia swarmed in his rear and cut off his supplies. The question now was how should he escape out of such an unfriendly wilderness and save his army from being surrounded and captured. After leaving the necessary garrisons at the captured posts, together with his losses and sick, he could scarcely count more than five thousand effective men, while Gates had ten thousand, mostly regulars, and the cry was, 'still they come.' Burgoyne, however, was supplied with the heaviest artillery and the best arms. He encamped on the plains of Saratoga, about three miles from Stillwater, where Gates lay. Here a council was called. If they remained where they were they would starve ; to retreat was perilous, they would inevitably be pursued. There was nothing but to try the fate of battle, and, if successful, push on for Albany. The British camp was overhung with gloom. The American camp was full of joy: they smelled the battle, they scented the victory. The British and their savage allies were detested for the horrible cruelties that had marked the path of their army ; the day of vengeance was at hand. Burgoyne discovered that Gates was posting troops in his rear to cut off retreat. His army was on half-rations ; it was battle or surrender.

"The battle-day came. The British fought gallantly. They were led by able officers, and their case was desperate ; they were inspired by despair. The Americans fought with their hearts full of triumph. On that day, it is told that Morgan and Arnold were maddened with the thirst for battle. Above the clash of arms and roar of cannon their voices rang, cheering on their men, who seemed to catch the spirit of their leaders. Arnold had pushed back the ranks before him upon their camp, and was preparing to enter their works, when a musket-ball disabled the same limb that was shattered on that fearful New Year's morning at the storming of Quebec. The British were dreadfully handled, night suspended the fearful wrestle of the two armies, though the Americans continued a random artillery firing into the enemy's camp. The British losses had been great in killed and wounded. They mourned greatly the loss of General Frazer, one of their ablest generals. They buried him in the darkness of night, amid the roar of American artillery, so near that 'every moment the balls spattered up the earth into the face of the officiating chaplain.' The British generals beheld their troops worn down with excessive toil, and abandoned by their Canadian and Indian allies. They saw them completely surrounded, and at the mercy of more than twice their numbers, lying constantly upon their arms, enduring a continual cannonade, and receiving even rifle and grape shot in every part of their camp. They were

besides on less than half-rations, and endured
all this without a murmuring word, while they
were daily sinking under their hard necessities.
Burgoyne called a final council, and while they
debated, American bullets pierced the tent
where they were assembled. They decided to
accept their destiny and surrender. On the
17th of October, 1777, the articles of capitulation were signed. The British were to 'march
out of camp with all the honors of war to a
named place, where they were to deposit their
arms and leave their artillery ; to be allowed a
free embarkation and passage to Europe, upon
condition of not serving again in America during the present war ; the officers to wear their
side arms, all private property to be retained,
and no baggage searched.' These were very
generous conditions when we consider how
completely the British were in our power ; and
General Gates also showed great delicacy in
ordering his army within their own lines, that
they might not witness the humiliation of
the English as they stacked their arms. The
sick and wounded also received every attention
and kindness among the victors, the more to
their praise, as at this very time they had received the news of horrible desolation, pillage,
and burning in some of the beautiful villages

on the lower Hudson by the British under Clinton.

"Gates immediately dispatched the tidings to Congress. On being introduced into the hall, the messenger said, 'The whole British army has laid down arms at Saratoga ; our own,

HORATIO GATES.

full of vigor and courage, expect your orders.' Congress voted thanks to General Gates and his army, and presented him with a medal of gold. The captive army was ordered to march for Boston. It passed through the ranks of the victorious army, drawn up for the purpose. 'The English expected to be scoffed at and insulted ; not an American uttered a syllable ; **a** memorable example of moderation and military discipline.'"

"Good for our side!" exclaimed Harry. "Never trample on a fallen foe ; it wouldn't be American manners."

"There's the tea bell," said little Stevey; "how is your appetite, Nannie?"

"Very good, I thank you, Stevey."

CHAPTER XVII.

Washington Loses Philadelphia—Grander in Defeat
than in Victory—Valley Forge—An Army of Heroes.

"WHAT did I give you as the date of
Burgoyne's surrender, children?"

"You said the terms were signed on
the 17th of October, 1777," answered Albert.

"Very true. While these important events
took place in northern New York, but yet before the surrender, let us see what goes on in
Washington's camp in New Jersey in August
of the same year. He dared not move from his
position until he could discover what Howe's
plan of summer campaign would be, and he was
in the best possible place to watch his movements. He concluded that Howe would either
go up the Hudson to co-operate with Burgoyne,
or make another attempt to capture Philadelphia. To do this he might march across
New Jersey as before, or he might embark on
board the fleet of his brother, Admiral Howe,
and, going round by sea, either ascend the Delaware to the city, or enter the Chesapeake Bay
sail to its head, disembark his army, and march

to the city. It was barely possible that he might contemplate an expedition still further south ; though this last was not probable, as the hot season was now far advanced. Washington, therefore, stood still until Howe should make his move.

" Fortunately for our cause, Howe could not rid himself of the ambition or delusion that the capture of Philadelphia was a military achievement of the very highest importance. He therefore declined to ascend the Hudson River to Burgoyne's aid, though he did dispatch General Clinton in that direction with a body of men to reduce some forts on the upper Hudson. That general took one or two posts, burned some villages, and plundered and ravaged the poor people. Howe thought by this to draw Gates off from Burgoyne, and also to deceive Washington, but he failed to do either. Howe at last embarked his army and stood out for sea. Washington ordered a strict watch all along the coast, and the first appearance of the fleet to be transmitted to him. After some days they were seen at the mouth of the Delaware. Still Washington did not move, as it might only be a maneuver. The fleet disappeared, and was not seen for several days. Washington thought it might be possible that

Howe would yet return to New York and ascend the Hudson. The reason he so strongly suspected Howe of this move was because it would have been his highest wisdom to do so. Had Washington been in Howe's position it was doubtless what he would have done, though it was what he ardently hoped Howe would not do.

"Some days after, the fleet sailed into the Bay of Chesapeake, and Washington was no longer in doubt concerning Howe's real intentions. He forthwith put his army on the march, and ordered the militia of Pennsylvania, Delaware, Maryland, and Northern Virginia to join him below Philadelphia. His army reached fifteen thousand men, not more than ten thousand of them regulars, the remainder being militia, some of whom had seen no service. Howe's army was about twenty thousand strong, heavily · equipped and armed. Washington took post behind the Brandywine Creek, some miles south and west of Philadelphia, and awaited the attack. September 11 was the battle-day. You all look very eager and happy, dear children ; of course, you expect me to tell you how handsomely Washington gained the battle."

"Yes, that is just what we are waiting to hear," said Nannie.

"I am sorry to tell you he lost it."

"Too bad!" ejaculated Harry. "And did they get into Philadelphia?"

"They did, indeed."

"I never could quite understand why Washington should have lost the battle of Brandywine," said Albert. "It was his best chance for a field victory."

"You must always consider the difference between trained soldiers, whose trade is war, and hastily gathered militia, who perhaps never stood in action before. The British arms were also every way superior. Howe planned and maneuvered admirably, and was well seconded by able generals, among whom the German, Knyphausen, showed here, as he did elsewhere, great military skill. Remember, too, that Arnold and Morgan were not there; Washington had magnanimously sent them to the aid of Gates. They were towers of strength in battle. Howe succeeded in deceiving Washington's aids, who brought him false intelligence. The battle was gained by ruse, that is, trickery, which, you know, is perfectly admissible in war. The fighting was good on both sides until the republican ranks gave way under the heavy masses of English and German infantry, chasseurs, grenadiers, and guards, that were successively hurled against them. The rout would have become general, and the defeat more disastrous, but General Greene, who, for admirable generalship, was only second to Washington, opened his ranks to let the fugitives pass through and then closed them again, and, facing the enemy, he covered the retreat, which was conducted in good order. The French officers who served under Washington particularly distinguished themselves for gallantry. The Baron St. Ovary was made prisoner, which was much regretted. Captain de Fleury had a horse killed under him in the hottest of the action. Congress gave him another a few days after. La Fayette received a painful wound in the leg, but refused to retire, continuing to cheer on his soldiers and rally the faint-hearted. Count Pulaski, a noble Pole, performed prodigies of valor at the head of his light horse. Congress conferred upon him the rank of brigadier-general."

"Albert," said Stevey, raising his little pale face off the pillow, "don't forget to set their names among your heroes; what a long list you'll have."

"I'll remember them, Stevey."

"Among our own troops the Virginians and Pennsylvanians especially distinguished themelves for gallantry. They could not save the battle, however, and the first news of the defeat vas brought into Philadelphia by straggling ugitives from the army, who arrived in small arties through by-ways and by short cuts. The lay following the whole army reached the city. Congress showed a fine courage in the face of o great a reverse, and continued their sittings n order to reassure the hopes of the people. n fact they made a light matter of it. To Vashington, the loss of the battle was doubtless bitter disappointment. If so he kept it in his eart. For the rest, he encouraged his soldiers, vith the kindness of a father gathered up the tragglers, and held his forces well in hand, ready or better fortune. Reinforcements joined him, nd on the 16th Howe, who had come up slowly, ncumbered with his sick and wounded, found he vanquished army again ready for battle.

"When both sides were prepared for action violent rain-storm prevented the battle. The uskets and cartridge-boxes of the Americans being illy constructed, their powder and rms were useless for the time. Washington ielded to necessity and fell back. Congress djourned to Lancaster with the public archives nd treasures. On the 26th of September, 1777, he British entered Philadelphia.

16

"Washington now calmly considered the position of affairs. He remembered·that the British once held Boston, and the conquest ended in disgrace. They had also captured New York, but beyond affording a good harbor for the fleet it had very little advanced their cause. Now the choice had been between risking the fate of the army and the loss of the capital. They were not to be compared. The preservation of his army meant the preservation of the cause for which they contended. The loss of one of their cities was small in comparison, even were it the capital. He, however, resolved to risk a surprise attack on the British camp at Germantown, a village near Philadelphia. It was made and failed, because of unforeseen difficulties that met them on their arrival ; the chief obstacle being a dense fog that hung over the camp, and prevented their seeing the enemy or directing their own movements with any certainty. The brave spirit of Washington bowed in humility before what seemed the decrees of Providence.

"He prepared to lead his army into winter-quarters. Congress saw the wisdom of the American chief. They sanctioned all his plans, conferring larger powers upon him than he had ever exercised heretofore, to do whatever he considered best for the cause in which they were alike interested. As for Howe and the British, they were exceedingly disappointed to find that the loss of their capital sat so lightly on the people. They were still undismayed and unconquered ; indeed, the British army found themselves close prisoners in the city, for Washington and his army hovered in the vicinity, protecting the country from plunder, capturing the enemy's foraging parties, and preventing supplies from going into the British camp. They had also obstructed the river so effectually that Admiral Howe could not ascend it to assist his brother, or furnish him with provisions. Howe at once addressed himself to the task of capturing the batteries on the shore, while the admiral proceeded to take up the obstructions in the river. With incredible trouble and a great deal of hard fighting they succeeded in taking the batteries and opening up a narrow ship channel to the city, and General Howe depended mainly on his brother to feed his army, with the assistance of the few tories who occasionally brought in supplies by stealth.

" Meantime Washington had selected for his quarters a place about twenty miles from Philadelphia, called Valley Forge, a rocky hollow among hills, where the soldiers built rude huts to screen them from the biting blasts. Washington spent here the dreariest, darkest, bitterest hours of his life. Howe and his army were the least of his foes. Heaven and earth seemed to be arrayed against him. Providence had been pleased to appoint him defeat instead of victory ; but a greater anguish wrung his heart, even the daily sight of his faithful soldiers battling with cold, hunger, nakedness, disease, and death. Some had not even straw to lie on. Their bed was the cold winter ground ; a very few had blankets. Some had one shirt, many none at all. Most were barefoot. They were poorly and irregularly fed. This brought disease. They had no comfortable hospitals, no invalid delicacies, and the noble fellows breathed out their lives by hundreds. It was Washington's fate to see all this misery, as the pale hand was stretched out to clasp for the last time that of the beloved commander, and the languid eye raised to catch his look of sympathy and tenderness."

"Why, what were the people about," asked Nannie with a tremulous voice, "that they didn't bring their blankets, and clothing, and every thing they had, for such soldiers ?"

"Well, my dear, it is impossible to keep an army supplied by private gifts and charities.

Give me your attention and I will explain some of the reasons for this suffering. As I told you before, the country was very poor in gold and silver ; all that could be obtained was sent abroad to buy powder, arms, and clothing for the army, for these were of the first necessity, and there were few of these they manufactured in our country at that time. For home money the Congress had issued paper bills, and each State also issued their own paper money ; but the people had not confidence in it ; they would not take it in exchange for provisions, or any thing they had to sell, if they could avoid it. You know the farmers were poor ; they depended upon the sale of their cattle and crops to support their families, and the British always paid them in gold tor whatever they bought. This was a great temptation to poor people, when they would rather have sold to the American army if they could have paid them. Often when provisions and clothing were ordered they did not arrive in time, and that caused great suffering. For instance, Harry, you had your dinner at the usual time to-day and ate heartily ; but I think you'll be quite ready for the supper bell."

" Yes, that I will, for I skated two hours on the pond this afternoon, and I just feel as if I hadn't eaten any thing for a week. I am as hungry as a bear."

" Well, suppose by some domestic catastrophe the next meal couldn't be furnished. Suppose that to-morrow morning, instead of buckwheat cakes and sausages, you were exhorted to content yourself with a small-sized crust without butter, and washed down with clear spring water ; at dinner a few beans, with the apology that the market wagon had broken down some miles away on a bad road ; and spiced with a promise of something really nice and hot for supper."

" Heart-rending !" exclaimed the hungry boy.

" Clothing, too, and blankets, which had been ordered for this winter from Europe, were much delayed by contrary winds, and want of transportation to the camp after they reached the country. All complaints and grievances were of course lodged with the commander-in-chief for final remedy. It was impossible for Washington to be military commander, commissary general, medical director, and, in short, *every thing;* yet all these cares in a measure came upon him. At last he ceased to expostulate with Congress upon these subjects, for he saw they were powerless to help him. They could recommend measures, but they could enforce nothing. He therefore wrote to the governors of the different States, as well as to influential individuals everywhere, urging them to relieve the sufferings of the starving perishing heroes of Valley Forge. This course brought relief at last, but not before they had endured untold sufferings with a patient and unmurmuring fortitude that ought to live in the memory of America down through all time.

" Washington also sent his thoughts and his influence beyond the seas in behalf of his country, thus adding to his labors the duties of foreign minister. He wrote to Benjamin Franklin, then envoy at the court of France, causing his views to be laid in full before the French king and his council, declaring that unless France would come at once to our aid the struggle could not be continued. Another evil that Washington contended with was the want of paper money, little worth as it was, to pay his soldiers and officers. Some of his officers had spent their private means, many were in debt, and could no longer keep up the appearance that became their rank and station in life. Able and brave men they were, who would gladly have served their country, but pride and self-respect compelled them to resign their commissions. This example was most pernicious to the common soldiers, and it required all of Washington's powers of persuasion and the influence of his character to prevent the dissolution of his army. He urged Congress to do something to meet this difficulty, and they did pass an act granting half pay to officers for life, and sent speedily all the funds they could command for present needs.

"But to crown all these trials, there were men who sought to drag down Washington's fame as a soldier and his ability as a commander ; who declared that the reverses of New Jersey and the loss of Philadelphia were owing to his incapacity. Anonymous letters were sent to him, also to the President of Congress and to the governors of several of the States. They extolled Gates for his great victory over Burgoyne, forgetting that his army outnumbered the British general's more than two to one, and that all the circumstances of the case were in his favor and against his enemy. One General Conway, a foreigner, was at the head of the intrigue, and they hoped to induce Washington to resign his commission, that Gates might be appointed in his stead.

"All these things came to Washington's knowledge. It did not disturb for a moment

the calmness of his lofty soul. Thoroughly devoted to the cause of his country, 'loving the
cause more than the honor of serving it,' he
forgot himself. He had no ambition, no self-
love, no vanity to wound. He wrote to Congress from Valley Forge, 'that neither interest
nor ambition had engaged him in the public
service ; that as far as his abilities had permitted
he had fulfilled his duty, aiming as invariably at
the object proposed as the magnetic needle points
to the pole ; that as soon as the nation should
no longer desire his services, or another should
be found more capable than himself of satisfying
its expectations, he should quit the helm, and return to private life with as much pleasure as
ever the wearied traveler retired to rest ; that
he wished his successor might experience more
propitious gales and less numerous obstacles ;
that if his exertions had not answered the expectations of his fellow-citizens, no one could lament it more than himself ;' but, he added, 'a day
would come when the interests of the country
would no longer require him to conceal truths,
while his silence now wronged himself.' Washington in these last words had allusion to ambitious men and dishonest contractors who had
contributed mainly to bring on his army the sufferings and calamities that I have told you of.

These were dark days to the Father of his Country ; often he was known to seek some solitude without the camp and wrestle in prayer with the God of battles ; for he refused to despair, and amid the storm he lashed his soul to God's promises and trusted on. In every earnest human life there come such crises, when the spirit of man fails before the greatness of the occasion, and the human arm is altogether too short to save. In these hours the soul may reach out through the darkness, and by faith lay hold of the powers of the world to come. Such extremity is ever God's opportunity ; but while he gives the victory, he teaches the lesson that no flesh may glory in his sight. Washington was not left to ' serve alone,' for God arose and scattered his enemies, and he stood in the midst of the people loftier, grander, and more beloved than ever."

CHAPTER XVIII.

The French declare openly for the American Cause— The British more anxious to get safely out of Philadelphia than they were to get into it—French Promises better than French Performances.

" IT is time, children, that we should look in upon our foes and friends across the waters."

"Yes, dear aunty, you have never told us what they said in England about Burgoyne's surrender."

" I will tell you this evening. As you may suppose, the king and his ministers, and all the enemies of America, were gloomy enough at such ill news. Burgoyne's army had been fitted out at vast expense, and their expectations were in proportion. They blamed General Howe very much because he did not obey instructions by going up the Hudson to Burgoyne's assistance, instead of leading his large and splendidly equipped army to the fruitless victory of the capture of Philadelphia, which, after all, became only snug prison-quarters for his soldiers, with Washington's army for their keepers. Howe, in turn, blamed them for not furnishing the promised re-inforcements in time, and asked leave to resign.

" The ministers accepted his resignation and appointed Clinton his successor. He was then with the army in Philadelphia. The hope of conquering the American people was dying out in England. They had gone to vast expense in raising the formidable armies they had sent out the year before under the leadership of the very ablest general the British army could boast. The results were worse than nothing, for their victories were turned into defeats, and their defeats were disastrous without remedy. The name of America was honored throughout Europe, while England's banners were hung with disgrace. In short, nobody wished them well. Still they would not give up the struggle ; they had a large force in America, and a great number of British war ships in our waters. They determined to hold out yet longer, hoping that the poverty and exhaustion of the Americans would compel them to submit. They knew well the poverty and the sufferings of the people and the armies, and expected to starve them out. The British ministers and the king were truly sorry they had ever undertaken this work of conquering America by force of arms. They would gladly give them now all, and more than all, the

rights and guarantees they had demanded before the war if they would only consent to come
again under British rule, and abandon the idea
of being an independent nation.

" But they repented too late. Parliament sent
commissioners to America to try to make terms
with them. They wanted, if possible, to treat
with the States separately, and so break up this
hated union, which was the rock of their ship-
wreck. The States refused to treat with them.
Congress would not admit them to an audience.
They then addressed themselves to influential
individuals, with no better success. They insulted General Reed by offering him £10,000,
and any office in the king's gift, if he would leave
the service of his country. The brave man gave
for answer, ' Poor as I am, the king of England
is not rich enough to buy me.'

" But let us look in now at the French court,
and see what hope was there for America. You
remember I told you that there was no real
sympathy for our cause with the French king
and his ministers. If they came to our aid it
would be not that they loved us, but that they
hated England. So it was with Spain and the
Dutch. They had all suffered in time past at the
hands of the English. England was stronger
than they, and used her strength without scruple.

Now they rejoiced that she was about to lose her most valuable possessions. In every nation we had many true sympathizers, for there is a kinship among heroes the world over. The French people were enthusiastic in praise and admiration of American valor, but the French government still hung back from declaring openly for our cause. Now Washington and Franklin and the Congress came wisely to the conclusion that they had heard enough of French promises, and they would force them to come to some decision. They suspected them of double dealing. They were most greedy after all manner of advantages of trade and commerce, seemed to be intent upon making all they could out of our misfortunes, and were full of diplomatic tricks. Franklin determined to fight them with their own weapons, and, seeking an audience with the ministers, informed them that if they did not at once declare for America, and assist her with their fleets and armies, Congress would proceed to open negotiations with England with a view to a reconciliation, as the British Parliament were willing to grant them favorable terms. This, as Franklin desired, frightened the French Government into action."

"Good," said Harry ; " if you're coming, come along."

" Yes, they were terrified at the thought of
their old enemy, England, regaining her valuable
colonies and her ancient power over them, and
at last, on the 6th of February, 1778, a treaty
was concluded between his most Christian Majesty Louis XVI., King of France, and the United
States of America. This treaty acknowledged
the independence of the nation, and recognized
her among the nations of the earth. After
many articles concerning trade and commerce,
the two nations engaged to assist each other
with good offices, counsel and arms. It was
agreed that neither party should conclude truce
or peace with England without the consent of
the other. They were not to lay down arms
until the independence of the United States
should be acknowledged by treaties that should
terminate the war. British pride was stung to
the quick when it was announced that France
had recognized the revolted subjects of England
as a nation. No greater insult, indeed, could be
offered by one friendly nation to another. The
heart of old England throbbed with new life, and
the spirit of the nation was aroused by this
French interference with her family quarrel.
In justice to themselves, they must at once declare war against France for so great an insult.
France, of course, expected this, but she felt her-

self now ready for it. So great was the indignation of England at these French proceedings that many members of Parliament would have been willing to acknowledge the independence of America, make peace with her, and turn the whole force of the kingdom against France.

"Upon hearing these opinions, that great old English statesman, Chatham—he who had pleaded the cause of the American colonies from the first oppressive act of Parliament until he retired from the ministry—he who had warned the king and the lords of Council of their folly and madness toward America—though bowed with age and infirmity, had himself carried into the House of Lords to raise his dying voice against the rending of the kingdom by giving up the American colonies. He still thought it possible to make an honorable peace with them, and retain them under British rule. Chatham had made England what she was ; he had raised her to a height of splendor never before reached. It was the work of his life, the fruit of his genius. Now, in his old age, he saw the fair fabric tottering to its fall. He concluded his speech with these words, the last of his life : 'My lords, I have made an effort beyond the powers of my constitution to come down to the House on this day to express the indignation I feel at an idea, which I understand has been proposed to you, of yielding up the sovereignty of America. My lords, I rejoice that the grave has not closed upon me ; that I am still alive to lift up my voice against the dismemberment of this ancient and most noble monarchy. Surely this nation is no longer what it was ! Shall a people that seventeen years ago was the terror of the world now stoop so low as to tell its ancient, inveterate enemy, France, Take all we have, only give us peace ! Let us at least make one effort ; and, if we must fall, let us fall like men !'

"To his argument it was replied by other members that the conquest of America by force of arms was impossible, and that it would be wiser to secure her friendship as an independent power than to throw her into the arms of France as an enemy. Chatham rose to reply, but he swooned and fell in his seat. The old statesman's heart was broken ; he never spoke again.

"Let us hope that to the dying eyes of this truly great man was revealed some vision of a kingdom that cannot be moved, whose foundations are in the heavens, whose king is all-powerful, all-wise, and all-good, and whose ministers do always his bidding.

"The tidings of the French alliance was

17

received with unbounded joy both in France and America. The French minister was welcomed with the profoundest respect and appropriate demonstrations, both by the American people and by Congress. Monsieur Gerard, the French minister, delivered his letters of credence, signed by Louis XVI., and directed to his ' Very dear great friends and allies, the President and Members of the General Congress of the United States of America.' Gerard accompanied these letters with a friendly speech, full of good hopes and wishes for the success of the two nations. The president of Congress, Henry Laurens, answered with great ease and dignity. The authorities of Pennsylvania, many strangers and eminent persons, officers of the army, and others, were present on this occasion. The national joy was without measure.

" The military plans of the British were necessarily entirely changed by these events. Orders were dispatched immediately to General Clinton to evacuate Philadelphia and take position again at New York. This was necessary because the French fleets were already afloat and steering toward the shores of America. It was feared that they would arrive in time to block up Admiral Howe's fleet in the Delaware, and that they should then have a more disastrous surrender than that of Burgoyne. England could afford no further reinforcements to America at this time, and even found it necessary to detach troops from America to strengthen her garrisons in the West India Islands, which they knew would soon be points of attack by the French navy. They also designed to move the seat of war from the Northern to the Southern States ; finally hoping to find, in the open fertile plains of the South, inhabited by the king's friends, a better field for their military movements, and some consolation for their disasters in the cold, mountainous, and difficult regions of the North, which swarmed with rebels. General Clinton would have embarked his army at Philadelphia on Howe's fleet and sent them round by sea to New York, but it was feared they might fall in with the French fleet. Nothing remained but to cross New Jersey, encumbered with their baggage and provisions, for they were not only going through an enemy's country, but also a country devastated and wasted by war, so that they could not depend upon it for supplies. The whole army passed the Delaware early on the 22d of June, 1778. Washington broke up his camp at Valley Forge, and put his army in motion. He ordered Morgan with his light horse to infest their skirts, trample on their heels, pick up their baggage, capture their stragglers, and annoy and harass them in every possible way." -

" Was that the Morgan who was with Montgomery in Canada ?" asked Nannie.

" The same. He was at the surrender of Burgoyne, too. Wherever danger was to be braved or glory won, we shall always find him."

" I hope he made it uncomfortable for them," said Harry. " I wouldn't have let them have as much as a blackberry by the way. I wonder Washington didn't pound them up, and be done with it."

" Easier said than done, my boy. British mortars and pounders were harder and better made than Washington's. Besides, it is impossible for one army to demolish another in battle. It is a game at which both must play. In exhausting your enemy you exhaust yourself, and the fighting stops from sheer exhaustion. It had been decided in council not to force a battle unless success seemed certain. They followed the enemy across New Jersey to Monmouth. The British moved slowly, encumbered with so much baggage, and excessively annoyed by Morgan. They lost a great many by desertion, especially of the Hessians. At Monmouth

Washington could no longer refrain from bringing on an engagement; but his orders were imperfectly carried out, especially by General Lee, who in council had voted against the attack. His troops gave way, and the tide of battle was turning against us, when Washington, who on this occasion 'was not master of his anger,' hurried to the rescue in person, addressed a sharp reprimand to Lee in the presence of his men, rallied the troops, and redeemed the fortunes of the day. Night closed with great advantage to the Americans. The men slept on their arms, intending to renew the battle on the morrow; but Clinton thought not, and wisely, under cover of darkness, stole away unperceived.

"The June heat (it was the 29th of the month) was excessive, and Washington thought it not prudent to give chase. Many of his men died from exhaustion after the battle of the previous day, and he ordered a day of rest and refreshment. Clinton pushed forward, and arrived at Sandy Hook, where Howe was waiting with his transports to take his army across to New York."

"Hurra, Stevey!" exclaimed Harry; "the king of France marched up the hill, and then marched down again. From New York to

Philadelphia, and from Philadelphia back to New York. I wonder how they liked it."

"They did not like it at all. The British were exceedingly mad against us, from King George down ; especially so, since the commissioners that the king had sent to America had utterly failed either to frighten, coax, or buy the patriots from their duty to their country. Before they left these shores they declared that henceforth the war would be carried on without mercy; and as the Americans had resolved to throw themselves into the arms of France rather than return to their allegiance to the mother country, they would so conduct the war as to ravage, plunder, and impoverish the land to the utmost, and thus make the prize less rich for their enemies, the French. They carried this out to the letter, as we shall see."

"How wicked and detestable of them," said Nannie.

"You remember I told you that war meant every form of barbarous cruelty and wrong. It is a fearful wickedness for a Christian nation to make war for any cause whatever. Defensive wars may be justifiable, after forbearance ceases to be a virtue. Happily, it is written, 'They that take the sword shall perish by the sword.' But, in any case, once 'let slip the dogs of war,' and you can have only anguish and desolation. Nothing less need be expected.

" Meantime the much-talked-of French fleet, under Count d'Estaing, had arrived, but, as it proved in the end, to very little purpose, as he and Admiral Howe played a game of ' hide and seek' all summer. D'Estaing came a few days too late to blockade the mouth of the Delaware. He then followed Admiral Howe to New York, and being in much better condition, with many more guns, ought to have attacked immediately. Though the English admiral knew he was in no condition to measure swords with his adversary, yet such was his English pride that he drew up his ships and bravely offered battle. This happy show of courage, together with an adverse tide, decided the French admiral to decline battle, and he sailed away toward Newport, a spacious harbor on the coast of Rhode Island, which the English had held almost from the commencement of the war, and which the Americans much wished to recover. If he had stayed a few days longer in the vicinity of New York, he would have been fortunate enough to pick up the war vessels of Admiral Byron, who had been sent from England to reinforce Howe, for a great storm met them on approaching the coast and separated them, so they straggled in one by one, and would have fallen an easy prey to the French fleet. But d'Estaing missed his opportunity. All Byron's ships came safely in at last, and Howe feeling himself quite a match for d'Estaing, went in search of him to bring him to battle.

"The Frenchman sailed boldly out of Newport harbor to meet the English fleet; but when, after a whole day's maneuvering to get the advantage of the wind, they were at last in position for battle, a violent gale set in, and a furious storm arose, and beat both French and English vessels about so roughly that they thought no more of fighting each other, but only of getting safely back to the harbors from which they had sailed. Here they were occupied for some time in refitting and repairing damages. Afterward d'Estaing had a fair chance to capture Newport, as the English fleet was greatly inferior to his own, and Washington dispatched General Sullivan to co-operate with him by land. At the last moment, when all was ready, the Americans having at great expense equipped the expedition, d'Estaing announced his intention to sail away to Boston harbor. The Americans protested against such a measure, and La Fayette besought him not to desert the cause at the moment when victory seemed

certain, as such conduct would have the effect
to disgust the Americans with their new
allies.

Notwithstanding these entreaties, he sailed
away at his own appointed time, August 23,
and reached Boston in three days. The Americans were very angry, and justly so, as it left
the land forces in great danger, especially as

GENERAL GREENE.

Admiral Howe came into Newport harbor as
soon as d'Estaing sailed out of it, for he was

still determined to give him a sound thrashing before he left for England. However, with much skill the American Generals Greene and Sullivan, with La Fayette, managed to bring off their forces without loss, though it was a very narrow escape. Howe then sailed away to Boston harbor after d'Estaing, but he had got safely into port, and Howe dared not pass the batteries to attack him. So he returned again to New York harbor after his fruitless chase, where he resigned his command to Admiral Byron, and returned to England."

" Well, I'm sorry he did not find him and give him a black eye for his trifling," said Harry.

" Not exactly," explained Albert, " remember the French and Americans are on the same side. If you whip them, you whip us."

"Admiral Byron, as soon as he was ready, started in search of d'Estaing to chastise him, but a tempest met him and damaged him so severely that he was obliged to put into Newport harbor, and d'Estaing took this opportunity to sail away from Boston, and take his course for the West Indies. Admiral Byron followed him as soon as he was able, to look after British interests in the Islands. At the same time Colonel Campbell with a British force was sent from New York to enter and overrun the State of Georgia. Thus early in the year 1779 the scene of war shifted suddenly from North to South.

CHAPTER XIX.

France, Spain, and Holland unite against England —She makes heroic resistance, but continues the war upon America with ferocity—The tide of battle flows Southward and the British take Charleston.

" WHAT was the situation last evening, Albert?"

" The French and English fleets had left our coasts and gone to the West India Islands, and a British army had landed at Savannah, Georgia, to make war upon the Southern provinces."

" The date?"

" January, 1779."

" Yes. We have also Clinton at New York, with the army he brought across New Jersey, besides full garrisons in all the New York defenses.

" For four years from this date the English and French fleets swept the seas in pursuit of each other ; Spain, and finally Holland, joined France against England, and their fleets were combined for her destruction. From looking

mean and contemptible, which a strong power
always does when oppressing a weak one, England looked grandly now, struggling with such
fearful odds. Even her foes respected her.
Their object was to destroy her power at sea,
where she had long domineered in every part
of the world, to the great disadvantage of the
other European powers. We cannot now follow these fleets in all the details of their movements. They were very much in this style :
France would seize an island belonging to England, soon England would seize one belonging
to France. Now the Spanish would fall upon
a convoy of English merchant ships coming into port, richly freighted, from the East Indies ;
again the English would catch a fleet of French
merchantmen, and then the French would capture a fleet of English merchantmen. Varying
from these thefts and high-sea robberies, the
fleets having met with wind and tide favorable for
action would come to battle, and batter and splin-
ter each other's vessels about equally. Splendid sea fights, they were, well set with valors,
heroisms, and magnanimities beautiful to read of,
and wounds, agonies, and deaths fearful to hear
of ; sometimes grappling their ships together,
fighting hand to hand, refusing to surrender,
and at the last ships and men going down to-

gether into the deep with their colors flying—
' There was sorrow on the sea,' in truth."

" O, aunty, do tell us about the sea fights, I
love to hear it," said Harry.

"Not now, Harry ; when I have leisure I will
read you some descriptions of them ; at present
I want to draw your attention to the fact that
though an over-ruling Providence suffered England to be chastised, crippled, and humbled,
yet he did not suffer her to be destroyed. The
combined fleets of France, Spain, and Holland,
though so much stronger, were not able to over-
whelm her. Once or twice heaven came to her
aid as by a miracle. Once the fleets of France
and Spain appeared off the coast of Great
Britain. They consisted of sixty-six ships of the
line, followed by a cloud of frigates, cutters, and
fire ships ; also a squadron of observation of sixteen ships of the line. Besides this immense
armada—one of the most formidable the ocean
had ever borne—three hundred transports were
in reserve on the coasts of France. Forty thousand men lined the shores of Normandy, well
equipped and drilled. They intended to make
a descent upon the English coasts. England's
doom seemed certain : she had a very small land
force, and her naval defense at this time was
thirty-eight ships of the line, under Admiral Sir

Charles Hardy. All that he could do was to stand off and on, near the mouth of the channel ; and his only hope was to entice the enemy into the narrowest part of the channel, where superiority of numbers would not avail him. But help came from heaven. North-east gales set in furiously, and drove and scattered this mighty naval armament ; and when the gales ceased, pestilence attacked the crews, and they were compelled to retire without effecting any part of their object. More than five thousand sailors died of the epidemic. At another time, when by a powerful combination the French and Spanish tried to break down her power, and the prospect was that she would be completely driven from the West Indies, having no visible strength to resist, a hurricane and plague again came to her aid, and saved her."

" But don't you think England deserved to be punished for her treatment to our Fathers ? " asked Nannie.

" She was well punished, my dear ; but it would have been a real calamity to the general interest of the world for England to have been overwhelmed by France and Spain. The English nation is a great and valuable nation. She is not always, perhaps never, adequately represented by her government. Governments often do foolishly and wickedly, and the people are wronged and shamed by it. If the English people could have voted whether they should go to war with America, it is not likely there would have been an American war. England has played a wise and great character in European affairs, and has been the bulwark of Protestant Christianity in Europe. I am glad that she was crippled and exhausted so that at last she was obliged to stop the war in America, and let our Fathers go in peace ; yet I am not only glad, but thankful, that Providence saved her from destruction by the Catholic powers of Europe.

"We must now return to our own country, and see what is taking place in Carolina. This sudden shifting of the war from the North to the South found the Southern provinces very illy prepared to resist the invasion. Colonel Campbell landed on the coast, near Savannah, and found the Americans drawn up for battle. The Hessians and Highlanders rushed to the attack with great impetuosity, easily breaking the ranks of the raw Carolina militia. The regulars were too few to restore the fortunes of the day, and soon dispersed. Savannah fell into the hands of the British, and, as there was no organized force to oppose them, they over-

ran the State, and took post at Augusta, in
order that they might assemble the tories,
the king's friends, who inhabited the upper
part of the country. Colonel Campbell, encouraged by so faint a resistance, sent a force into
South Carolina to capture the harbor of Port
Royal ; but the South Carolina patriots made
so good a defense that the enemy were forced
to retire.

" Meantime the tories in the upper part of the
States of Georgia and South Carolina had assembled, and were marching to join the British
at Augusta ; but the militia under Colonel
Pickens having once more found their courage,
intercepted them, and after a sharp fight the
tories were routed, leaving their leader and a
large number dead upon the field. The British,
discouraged by this disaster, left Augusta and
retreated to Savannah, and kept themselves
near their ships for safety. Washington felt a
great anxiety for the Southern States, but was
unable to move to their relief. He sent, however, General Lincoln, a man much esteemed by
the Southern people. Encouraged by his presence and efforts the militia again assembled in
considerable numbers, but before Lincoln could
prepare his forces for battle the British attacked and routed him at Briar Creek. Push-

18

ing their advantage, they stole quietly along the coast into South Carolina, hoping to surprise and capture Charleston, but the patriots of that State stood well upon their guard, and the British retired again into Georgia. They now suspended regular warfare until the summer heats should pass and reinforcements from New York should arrive. Meanwhile they spent the time, especially those German barbarians, the Hessians, in plundering every thing they could carry away, and in destroying all they could not take.

" You remember the British had given notice that henceforth the war should be for their destruction and wasting. Let us see what they were doing at the North at this time. Clinton had sent a considerable force by sea, to land upon the coast of Virginia at Norfolk, where supplies were abundant at this season. There was none to oppose them, for Washington could not spare a man to the defense of his native State, because Clinton was at this very moment threatening the most important military posts on the Hudson. So they plundered and stole to their heart's content, loading their vessels with provisions and tobacco, which was exceedingly valuable, and with many thousand barrels of meat, just salted and ready to be sent to

Washington's army. They burned houses and vessels, and left that beautiful country one vast plain of smoking ashes.

"Returning to New York to discharge their booty and receive fresh orders, they were directed to ravage the coast of Connecticut. This coast was full of convenient harbors that sheltered the American privateers with their prizes. Privateers are armed vessels that range the seas in search of their enemy's ships. Congress had authorized this species of high-sea robbery —for it is nothing less, though it is done by all maritime powers in war. These privateers were swift sailers, and being no match for the English war vessels, they hung along the coast on the watch for English transports bringing provisions and supplies to the British army. They pounced upon their prey, and ran with it into any of these little coast harbors. In this way many a rich prize was secured."

Harry thrummed on the table and sang :

" Will you walk into my parlor, said the spider to the fly,
It is the prettiest little parlor that ever you did spy."

He excused himself for the interruption by saying that he did it to wake Stevey up, who seemed to be going to sleep. But little Stevey opened his brown eyes very wide, and said he had heard every word, but it rested him more to lie with his eyes closed.

Aunt Edith continued: "The British were determined to break up these sea-robbers' haunts, and they stalked along the coast like destroying demons. They spared nothing. Village after village was laid in ashes, hundreds of vessels were burned, and every excess and cruelty committed. And now we will go up the Hudson and see what was doing there. You perhaps remember that at the time Burgoyne had found himself in such a critical condition, and sent earnest entreaties to Howe to come up the Hudson to his relief, that general did dispatch General Clinton in that direction, to draw Gates' attention from Burgoyne. Clinton took several strong posts, among them Stony Point. Washington much regretted the loss of this place, and now determined at this time to attempt its recovery; the more so as the English had since strengthened it by every military art, until it had become a formidable fortress. It had a large garrison, and vast quantities of stores of all kinds. Washington charged General Wayne with the recapture of this place, and provided him with a strong detachment of the most enterprising spirits of his army. Wayne was a tornado in battle; his enthusiasm amounted to intoxication, so that he had won the name of Mad Anthony! The party set out July 15, 1779; the way lay over 'high mountains, difficult defiles, deep morasses, and roads narrow and bad.' They arrived at nightfall within a mile of the fort, and Wayne proceeded very quietly and cautiously to reconnoiter the works. They were not observed by the garrison. 'Wayne formed his corps in two columns, and put himself at the head of the right. It was preceded by a vanguard of picked men, commanded by the brave Fleury. This vanguard was itself led by a forlorn hope of twenty men, under Lieutenant Gibbon.'"

"What is a forlorn hope, aunty?" asked Alice.

"Those who go into battle never to come out. Of this forlorn hope of twenty, only three survived. The other column was led by Major Stewart, with a forlorn hope under Lieutenant Knox. They were ordered to march in silence with unloaded muskets, for they must win their way with fixed bayonets. At midnight they charged the defenses of the fort. 'The English opened a tremendous fire of musketry and cannon, but neither the double palisade, nor the bastioned ramparts, nor the storm of fire, could arrest the Americans; they opened the way with their bayonets, scaled the fort, and the two columns met in the center of the works. A musket-ball grazed Wayne's skull. He fell, but, rising on one knee, exclaimed, 'Forward! my brave fellows, forward!' He thought himself mortally wounded, and requested his aids to assist him forward, as he wished to die in the fort! The garrison surrendered with a loss of six hundred killed and prisoners. By command of Washington the fort was demolished and all its stores brought away. This brave achievement was a theme of praise throughout the land. Wayne received from Congress a medal of gold, Fleury and Stewart one of silver, and to the brave soldiers a sum of money was distributed equal to the value of the military stores taken.

"Let us look southward again in the fall of this same year 1779. Count d'Estaing, who had spent the summer in the waters of the West Indies, had received letters from the American authorities bitterly complaining of his conduct. They charged upon him the wasted expense of the expedition to Newport, and the loss of Savannah and all Georgia for the want of his co-operation; while he had been busy enriching France with the valuable conquest of the Islands of Dominica, St. Vincent, and Grenada, leaving his allies to fight their battles alone. He therefore resolved to bring his fleet to the rescue, and co-operate with Lincoln in the effort to retake Savannah. He arrived before Savannah in September, but finding it in an admirable state of defense, it was necessary to enter upon a regular siege. By the 9th of October the ardent Frenchman, in council with Lincoln, who commanded the American forces, ordered the assault. It was bravely made, but the defense was not less so. Forty French officers and seven hundred soldiers were killed and wounded. Among the wounded officers was d'Estaing. The Americans lost four hundred killed and wounded, among them the noble Pole, Count Pulaski. He left a name revered throughout America, and Congress ordered him a monument. The city remained to the British, with very little loss on their side. The news of this disastrous failure was received with profound sorrow at the North, and the only consolation that remained was the fact that the British, fearing lest d'Estaing might return to the attack on Newport or New York, and not being strong enough to defend both points, evacuated Newport, in order to make the defense of New York successful. Thus they were frightened away without real cause, and went very hurriedly, leaving much artillery and stores behind.

"Thus closed the year 1779, and 1780 opened with new disasters for our Southern friends ; for General Clinton, leaving a strong garrison for the defense of New York in his absence, embarked with a large land and naval force for the purpose of capturing Charleston. They succeeded in effecting a landing between the city and its sea defenses. Thus cut off, Fort Moultrie, which had made so gallant a resistance four years before, was now compelled to surrender. The American army was surrounded and overpowered near Charleston, their artillery and baggage were taken, with a large number of prisoners. Clinton then laid siege to the defenses of the city. Thus cut off from reinforcements and supplies, after a siege of forty days, Lincoln surrendered the city with his garrison, May 12, 1780."

"'Hail! horrors, hail!'" exclaimed Albert.

"Indeed, not since the fall of Ticonderoga had such a reverse befallen the American arms. The garrison included seven general officers, six thousand men, four hundred pieces of artillery, and military stores."

"I hope the seven general officers were put on the retired list," said Harry, indignantly.

"I should very much like to know whose fault it was."

"There was a very loud outcry, I assure you, and blameful charges laid here and there. These disasters were, however, not without their good results ; but I will reserve these for to-morrow evening's story."

CHAPTER XX.

" WE are to hear this evening what good came of British victories in the South," said Albert.

" Yes ; it waked the nation up out of a deep sleep that had fallen upon it. Ever since the alliance between France and America our countrymen had seemed to abandon themselves to the idea that their independence was accomplished ; their sacrifices and toils they thought were over. Washington saw this delusion with deep anxiety, and felt that if some remedy was not found, it might result in the utter failure of the revolution at the very moment when its ripe fruits were just within reach. The war had already dragged its slow and sorrowful length through four years. The sufferings and privations of the people were extreme ; there was also want of money, for the paper money of the country had scarcely any value by this time. This made it impossible to feed, clothe, and pay the army ; men would not enlist with such a threefold prospect of death from sword, naked- ness, and famine.

" Washington sent out his warnings and ex- hortations to Congress, State Legislatures, and individuals throughout the land. Still they seemed to sleep, but the disasters at the South waked them out of their sleep, and a fresh tide of enthusiasm swept over the country. Con- gress sent encouraging promises to the patriots of the South, who were now hiding among their hills and fastnesses, to keep the standard waving, and they should shortly have assistance both of men and money. The Southern people were suffering the most terrible barbarities from the British soldiery ; no mercy was shown them. Tarleton, a British officer who tracked the beau- tiful Carolinas in fire and blood, was especially noted for his cruelty. The patriots showed the noblest constancy. Many of the best men in the State were gibbeted for no other crime than faithfulness to the cause they called right. The women displayed the most heroic spirit, consol- ing their brothers and husbands in their gloomy dungeons, and exhorting them to stand to their principles. There could scarcely be said to be an American army in the State since the capit- ulation of Charleston ; but the militia wandered among the hills in small bands, and annoyed the enemy to the best of their ability.

"The most famous of these militia bands was that led by Colonel Sumter, a man greatly esteemed in the community for great military genius, and idolized by his men. The militia of both Carolinas hastened to join him. They had no pay, no uniforms, and many of them no clothing at all—I mean what I say—not a garment. Some of them had only moss and leaves to prevent the friction of their straps and cartridge boxes against the bare skin. They often breakfasted on blackberries, dined on green corn, and supped on the remembrance of their dinner. Many of them were without arms, and in time of battle they waited aside, until wounds, or exhaustion, or death, disabled their comrades, when they seized their arms and stepped into the ranks to fill their places. These brave men held up their country's banner until the cause was again represented by continental troops that Washington dispatched from Virginia, Maryland, and Delaware, under General Gates, to the rescue of the South.

"Roused by the heroic endurance of their Southern brethren, a new spirit animated the men and women of the republic. In Philadelphia a society of ladies was organized for the purpose of furnishing clothing and supplies for the soldiers, and Mrs. Washington presided at its meetings. The ladies of other cities followed this example, and every one contributed something of money or labor. Some wealthy and influential capitalists also established a public bank. Subscriptions and loans poured in from every quarter, and the funds were kept entirely to meet the want of the soldiers in the field. About this time also La Fayette returned from France, whither he had gone on a visit, and to advance by his influence the interests of America. He announced the sailing of seven ships of the line, with a number of transports, bringing six thousand soldiers, which might now be hourly expected in American waters. They soon after made their appearance at Newport, and, to crown the satisfaction of the people, Washington was declared, by appointment of the French court, Commander-in-chief of the French forces while they remained in America. A new loan of specie from France was received at this time, and the six thousand French soldiers—careless of expense, as soldiers generally are—scattered their French coin in American shops. All these things afforded sensible relief to the country, but the tide of disaster at the South had not yet turned.

" Hearing that Gates, the hero of Saratoga, was advancing into the interior of South Carolina, and that he had menaced the fortified posts of the British, Lord Cornwallis, who commanded the British forces, advanced to meet him. The two armies encountered at Camden, near the center of the State. Gates did not display the prudence and ability that was expected of him, as he allowed Cornwallis to force a battle in a position very unfavorable to the Americans. They outnumbered the British, but from the nature of the ground only a small number could operate at one time, and the advantage of numbers was lost. The consequence was the most disastrous reverse that had ever befallen the American arms. Indeed, the honor of the republican cause was only saved by the gallantry of the Maryland and Delaware regulars, led by Generals Gist and Smallwood, under Baron de Kalb. The Americans lost two thousand killed, wounded, and prisoners, eight pieces of cannon, baggage, and stores. The British lost only about three hundred. It was August of 1780. Gates lost on the field of Camden much of the fame he had won on the plains of Saratoga. Three days after the battle the brave Baron de Kalb, a prisoner, mortally wounded, expressed with his dying breath his high sense of the valor displayed by the troops of Maryland and Delaware, declaring the satis-faction he then felt in having fallen in defense of a cause so noble and to him so dear. The Congress ordered that a monument should be erected to him at the city of Annapolis, the capital of Maryland.

" The fugitive army retreated into North Carolina for safety, and the banner of the re-public was no more seen except with Sum-ter's band of wild men of the woods, now here, now there, alternately pursuing and flying, and always keeping the British in terror."

" Why, aunty, Sumter was a guerrilla," said Nannie.

" Yes, just as Washington was among the hills of New Jersey ; both doing the best and wisest things possible under the circumstances.

" While these shameful tidings came from the hills of South Carolina, a scene was enacting amid the beautiful hills of the Hudson that filled the land with horror and indignation. There was a scheme so skillfully planned, and so adroitly executed up to the final moment, that, but for the watchful eye of Him whose angels keep the gates of a righteous cause, would have brought to nothing the labors, sufferings, and glorious achievements of our Fathers."

Little Steve crept down from the lounge, and climbed into the chair beside Aunt Edith, and the children looked very much as children do when about to hear a ghost story ; but Albert said, " You are going to tell us about Benedict Arnold the traitor."

"Yes, would you believe it ! the man who led that band of heroes through the wilderness into Canada ; who afterward led them through the blinding hail storm of that fatal New Year's eve, 1775, scaled the walls of Quebec and was borne from the place of his brilliant but useless victory with a shattered limb ; the same Arnold who on the plains of Saratoga had fought with more than human inspiration, until, in the moment of triumph, a grievous wound in the same limb checked his career and appointed him weary months of pain. No braver man than Arnold ever led men to battle ; but it was physical courage spurred on by self-love. He was not brave of soul, for he was in bondage to the baser part of his own nature. Conquering others, he was himself a slave to his own passions and love of gain."

" O what a pity he didn't die with Montgomery on that New Year's morning !" exclaimed Nannie.

" Yes," added Harry, " then we should always

have loved him, and I don't like to hear any thing against him."

"Just as you feel, so our Fathers and Mothers felt. He was the nation's idol—the maimed, battled-scarred hero—and that was his ruin. He drank their idolatry until it intoxicated him. Being disabled from his wounds, Congress gave him a position at Philadelphia with full pay, without active service. Here he established himself in princely splendor, at enormous expense, which he could not afford. He speculated and gambled. Ill luck overtook him, and he found himself entangled in a net of difficulties. He was too proud to diminish the splendor of his living. Instead, he resolved to defraud the treasury of the nation, by presenting false accounts, which his position gave him the opportunity to do."

"Ah! that wasn't brave," said Harry, sorrowfully.

"That is so, Harry. Arnold was a coward. The man who had braved cannon ball and steel, and had borne the marks of both on his body, was a coward now when the battle was no longer one of brute force, but a moral encounter between right and wrong. His frauds after a time were detected. He was tried by court-martial, and sentenced to be reprimanded by

19

Washington. A very mild punishment certainly, but his pride could not brook it. In the
depths of his evil nature he swore revenge, but,
hiding his real feelings, he expressed a desire
once more to enter into active service, asked for
the command at West Point on the Hudson,
and received ˙it. These fortified posts on the
Hudson River were of the first importance.
The possession of them had been the object of
the British since the beginning of the war.
Burgoyne had for his final object the capture
of these points. It was to watch and guard
them that Washington lingered in their vicinity ;
nor could the distant disasters of the Carolinas,
nor the desolation of his own State, tempt him
to leave the defenses of the Hudson.

"Of these the strongest was West Point. It
had been fortified until it was pronounced the
Gibraltar of America. This place Arnold had
engaged to deliver into the hands of General
Clinton. He also promised to so divide and
post his men that they would fall an easy prey
to the British general. This done, Clinton could
readily surprise in detail the army of Washington, which was posted at various points on both
banks of the river. It would have involved the
loss of the army, and all the artillery and stores
which were deposited here as the safest military

magazine the country could afford. The traitor was to receive in return the same rank in the British army that he now held from the American Congress, with large sums of gold. The negotiations between Clinton and Arnold were carried on by one of Clinton's aids, Major Andrè, a young British officer, the admiration of all who knew him, for his gifts of mind, virtues of soul, and graces of person. A last interview was necessary to complete arrangements and sign the papers. Major Andrè reached West Point in safety, and concluded the whole affair. When about to return, Arnold insisted for his greater safety that he should take a citizen's dress ; hitherto he had worn his British uniform under an overcoat. Andrè did not want to do this, but yielded at last to Arnold's persuasions. He set off, and passed in safety all the posts of the American lines, and was within sight of the first British outpost, when he was challenged by three soldiers of the militia, ' who happened to be there,' says the historian ; but it appears to me, children, they were there by commission from the eternal council chambers of the God of nations to arrest Major Andrè. He offered them gold, his watch, and rewards and rank in the British army, if they would release him. Not they. John Paulding,

David Williams, and Isaac Van Vorst, were found incorruptible. Thus in the moment when one of the most distinguished chiefs of the American army, a man celebrated throughout the world for his brilliant exploits, betrayed, out of base vengeance, the country he had served for a purse of gold, three common soldiers stood faithfully to that country's cause, and refused to receive a bribe.

"Every effort was made by Arnold and the British to prove that Andrè was not a spy. They did not stint falsehood and duplicity to accomplish this. Unfortunately, it was necessary for Major Andrè to sustain them by lying also, and this he refused to do. He charmed his judges, and indeed all men, by his candor and greatness of soul. General Clinton loved him as a son, and suffered anguish at the thought of the fate that awaited Andrè as a spy. He offered to exchange a number of officers of high rank for him, but the laws of war sentenced him to death by hanging. Many conferences were held by officers on both sides, for so great was the interest felt, even by Americans, in this noble and youthful victim, that Washington allowed every evidence to be weighed in his favor; but the conclusion was irresistible that he was a spy. It was one of the saddest duties that

Washington ever performed. The young Englishman died as bravely as he had lived, and
many a heart sighed for him on both sides of
the Atlantic.

"Arnold escaped, and received the gold and
the rank; but the British loathed him as the
chief cause of the disgraceful death of the man
they idolized."

CHAPTER XXI.

The Morning Seems to Dawn—Heaven Sends the
Elements to Help—Hard Fighting in the Carolinas—
Many Defeats which Invariably turned out to be
Victories.

"THIS evening, children, we must go back
to the Carolinas, which we left, you remember, in some trouble."

"Yes, we remember only too well the battle
of Camden," answered Albert.

"The results were disastrous indeed; the
two Carolinas were once more at the mercy,
I should like to say, but I must needs say, at
the wrath, of Cornwallis and his bloodthirsty
General Tarleton. The deeds of violence and
cruelty perpetrated all over these States are
too horrible to tell. The British army was
posted through both States, and they lived by
the plunder of the people. Washington beheld
with anguish this state of affairs, as well as
the desolation and pillage of his own State,
but duty held him to his post on the Hudson. He recalled General Gates, and sent
to the Southern patriots his right and left

hands, in the persons of Generals Greene and Morgan."

"What! Canada Morgan?" asked Harry.

"Yes, and Saratoga Morgan, and Monmouth Morgan."

"I hope we'll begin to see better times down South," said Nannie.

"We shall. This General Morgan was every whit as brave a man as Arnold; put his name among your heroes, Albert, for he was as true as he was brave. In council Greene had no superior save only Washington, whom he loved to devotion, and whose tactics he had well studied. In battle, Morgan had no superior— no equal except Arnold, and he was under England's banner now, putting the torch to Virginia's homesteads and wasting her fair fields. Lord Cornwallis, who commanded all the British forces in the South, believing that the Carolinas were completely conquered, was instructed from England to push his victories into Virginia, where he would be joined by land and sea forces which Clinton would send from New York, and thus it was thought an easy conquest would be made of Virginia. With these three important States wrested from the armies of Congress, there was little doubt that the Americans would give over the struggle and close the war. The ministers of King George were now as much elated by their successes in the South as they had been when Burgoyne had accomplished the capture of Ticonderoga and the lake defenses of New York, and their expectations were as sanguine of the final triumph of Cornwallis as they had been of that of Burgoyne. Let us see. When Cornwallis heard that Morgan and Greene were arrived in North Carolina he made ready to meet them. Morgan, with his famous sharpshooters, was operating with Sumter and Marion, gathering up the fugitive militia, who had gone to their homes in despair after the disaster of Camden. He was also joined by Colonel Washington, with a body of light horse. Greene was at another point, drilling such material as he had, and waiting for the reinforcements that Washington had ordered to his support from Virginia, Maryland, and Delaware. Cornwallis sent the fierce, cruel, and hitherto unconquerable Tarleton to make a speedy end of Morgan, while he in person should advance and deal Greene a blow.

"Tarleton wanted immediate battle; Morgan did not, he therefore maneuvered for delay, until finding himself in good position he halted for battle. Tarleton made one of his usual furious onslaughts.   Morgan was seemingly everywhere at once ; his presence was an inspiration. He was ably seconded by Colonels Howard, Washington, and Pickens.   The battle raged ; now fortune seemed to incline to Tarleton, and now to Morgan, until, gathering all his forces, Morgan led a general charge upon the English lines.   The shock was tremendous ; they gave way and fled, the Americans pursued, and it became a rout.   Tarleton lost eight hundred men, cannon, baggage, and colors.   This was Morgan's battle of Cowpens, fought January, 1781."

The children clapped their hands and said they thought it was a good beginning for the New Year.

" Cornwallis heard of this defeat with dismay. He wished to retrieve it by a hasty attack upon Morgan before he could join his forces to those of Greene ; if successful, he could afterward follow and attack Greene.

Morgan was a good guesser.   Expecting this blow from Cornwallis, he had started his prisoners, baggage, and artillery forward, and followed with such good speed that he crossed the Catawba, and from its right bank saw Cornwallis approaching.   He had not crossed a moment too soon.   Providentially, a heavy rain fell, and the fords swelled so rapidly that the British could not attempt to pass the river."

"What is a ford?" asked Stevey.

"It is a shallow part of a stream which at low water allows a passage on foot. Greene, who had advanced to meet Morgan with part of his force, now took command, having directed the remainder of his army to join him higher up, at Guilford Court-House in North Carolina. Cornwallis wished to strike a blow before they could reach this point and join forces. The English pursued with hot haste, wishing to revenge the shame of Cowpens ; they even destroyed their wagons, part of their artillery and private baggage, and took as little provisions as they could, so that they might be unincumbered. But the Americans outran them, and made good the passage of the Yadkin, drawing all the boats after them. The English arrived only in time to see their adversary safely across. They would have followed immediately, but Heaven sent another sweeping rain storm from the hills above, and so swelled the river that they could not cross."

"How wonderful it was, aunty," said Nannie, "such plain, unmistakable deliverance for our Fathers just in the time of their great extremity."

"It makes me think of Daniel with the lions, and the three children in the furnace," added Stevey, "and God sending his angel to deliver them."

"It was exactly the same, dear Stevey; the same faithful, unchangeable God, the same yesterday, to-day, and forever; who never slumbers nor sleeps, but who watches and works with his faithful servants who have his cause in their keeping. He may sometimes suffer them to be hard pressed in the fight; they may even be cast down, but they shall not be destroyed. Many a tribute of praise went up from American hearts for these special providences, without which defeat must inevitably have befallen them, as Cornwallis was in much greater strength. Greene did not wish to fight until all his forces were united, and, indeed, not then if maneuvering would answer instead. Cornwallis thus far had been completely outgeneraled. He had expected to fight Morgan before he could join Greene, and afterward to attack Greene before he could unite his forces. It was for this he had suffered the destruction of his wagons, artillery, stores, and baggage, and carrying scant rations withal, to which his officers and soldiers submitted with admirable patience; but it was all lost. Every part of his plan had failed thus far. Do you remember Cornwallis' object, Albert ? "

" His instructions were to go to Virginia to join such forces as Clinton would send there by sea to assist him to subjugate that State."

"Well answered. Washington had penetrated these designs, and he had also dispatched a considerable force thither under La Fayette. Now Cornwallis did not want to take Greene with him to Virginia ; he wanted to fight in Carolina and demolish Greene's army. But Greene was determined to go to Virginia if Cornwallis went, for he knew that he would find reinforcements there. The question was now between the two generals who should get to Virginia first.

" The Roanoke River separates the States of North Carolina and Virginia, and the upper part of it, where it is fordable for an army, is called the Dan. Both armies started in full chase for this upper ford. The English put forth incredible efforts, and reached it first ; they rejoiced greatly, for they thought they had fairly caught Greene ; they would now force him to battle and beat his army into small dust, thus revenging the shame of Cowpens and the failure at Catawba and the Yadkin. Greene's position was indeed critical, but he summoned all the resources of his genius, though there was but one hope, namely, to cross at a lower ford. He turned and made for Boyd's Ferry, not knowing whether he would find it fordable or not. He pushed on at high speed, felling trees and breaking bridges behind him to delay the enemy, who were closely following.

" Leaving his cavalry and some light infantry to block up the roads, Greene pressed forward with the artillery and baggage. Reaching the ford, he found it passable, and also found some boats, which much assisted him, so that he crossed safely with all his effects. Even the gallant rear guard of cavalry, which had done such good service, made a safe passage of the river, and when Cornwallis and the British came panting up on the Carolina side, Greene and his followers saluted them in military style from the Virginia side."

" The top of the morning to you, Mr. Cornwallis," said Harry, bowing low and pulling a lock of his hair.

" He was a live lord, please remember," said Albert.

" His title didn't help him much through the pine logs and over the broken bridges," returned Harry.

" The disappointment and vexation of the

British general were extreme. All their fatigue and sufferings and losses counted nothing. They were outgeneraled, and did not dare at present to trust themselves in Virginia. Instead of this, he established himself in North Carolina, and sent his right arm of terror, General Tarleton, through the State, to overawe the republicans, stir up the king's friends, and bring as many of them as possible to enlist, and swell the numbers of his army.

" But Greene, who had received further reinforcements, did not intend to let Cornwallis and Tarleton desolate North Carolina as they had done South Carolina; so he boldly recrossed the Dan and threatened Cornwallis with attack. He advanced and took post at Guilford Court-House, and, having received still other reinforcements, resolved to accept a battle if offered. Cornwallis knew he could not venture into Virginia without giving Greene battle on this side, and he could not much longer remain in an enemy's country, encumbered with his sick and wounded, without proper supplies. It was therefore necessary for him either to come to battle or retreat, and accordingly he advanced to Guilford Court-House. Greene outnumbered him two to one. Cornwallis' force was not quite three thousand,

Greene's was six thousand. One half of these, however, were ill-armed militia. The battle opened skillfully on the part of the English. After one fire of muskets they charged the Carolina militia with bayonets, and they at once fled.

" O brother ! " said Harry impatiently, " what ailed the Carolina militia ; they always ran away before they fought."

" Touch them lightly Harry ; they were brave fellows, and did splendid guerrilla service. If they ran away one day, they were sure to come back the next, and were always ready to ' pick their flint and try it again.' They were really not fit for open field service, with only bird guns and rusty old firelocks. Is it wonderful that they could not stand against the burnished steel and artillery of these heavy ranks of European soldiers who had literally lived in battle ? Then, of all things, a bayonet charge is the severest test of a soldier's firmness."

" That's so," added Albert. " To stand a bayonet charge is something a soldier has to learn. I don't wonder they ran."

" Well, what next, aunty," asked Nannie, anxiously.

" Why, General Stevens, who commanded in their rear, seeing the confusion, assured his men that they had been instructed to fall

back after the first fire, and they must open
their ranks and let them pass, then close up
promptly after them. This saved the battle in
this part of the field, but it raged furiously
right and left. Victory, hovering above the
standards of both armies, declined to fold her
wings on the banners of either ; it ended a
drawn battle, though the British boasted a great
deal, and called it a victory. The battle of
Guilford Court-House took place March 15,
1781. They did hold the battle-field, but their
loss in killed and wounded was greater than ours,
so that Greene took strong position a few miles
away, and was better prepared to renew the battle than the British general, who was so encumbered with his sick and wounded, and pinched
for supplies, that his situation had become critical. In council with his officers it was thought
prudent to retreat to Wilmington, where their
fleet were at anchor and could furnish the supplies they so much needed. So again the victors fled before the vanquished.

"Instead of following Cornwallis to Wilmington, Greene, seeing that North Carolina was
now free from the presence of the British,
pushed boldly on toward South Carolina, whose
inhabitants still lay exhausted beneath the cruel
power of their foes. Cornwallis had left small

garrisons at Camden, Ninety-six, Augusta, and other fortified places, all under command of Lord Rawdon. Greene advanced toward Camden, but found it too well fortified to attempt an assault. He fortified himself on the heights, about a mile away, named Hobkirk's Hill. Lord Rawdon attacked him here, and after a sharp battle Greene fell back some miles. This was another British victory, though my Lord Rawdon, a few days after, found it best to destroy the fortifications at Camden, and fall back toward the sea-coast, as far down as Eutaw Springs. Meantime, Colonels Pickens and Clarke, with their militia, were knocking at the gates of Ninety-six and Augusta. The latter surrendered with its garrison to Colonel Pickens, and the garrison of Ninety-six were ordered to evacuate that post and join Lord Rawdon. Greene pursued him to Eutaw Springs, and the 8th of September, 1781, witnessed a hard-fought battle here. The British called it a victory again ; but the American Congress voted Greene a medal of gold and one of the Congress standards, and the British shortly after withdrew from every part of the State, and shut themselves up within the intrenchments of Charleston.

" Thus ended the campaign of the South, and

thus, after two years of hard, stubborn fighting, the whole fabric of British power in the Carolinas fell to pieces."

"And where was Cornwallis all this time," asked Harry.

"I'll tell you to-morrow evening."

CHAPTER XXII.

Surrender of Cornwallis to Washington—Peace.

"HOW unfortunate we are!" exclaimed Nannie, entering the library. "There is a letter from the manor, saying that Aunt Rachel is sick, and Alice and Aunt Edith are to go the day after to-morrow, and nobody can tell when they'll be back."

"Well, at all events let us get to our places, for I think we'll hear the end of Cornwallis to-night," said Albert. "Here comes Aunt Edith now."

Being seated, she inquired where they had left Cornwallis last evening.

"At Wilmington, where he found it necessary to retreat after his brilliant victory at Guilford Court House," said Harry.

"Yes. Here he called a council of officers, for they had come to the parting of the ways. Cornwallis must either chase Greene back through South Carolina, or push through North Carolina into Virginia, and execute his long-baffled plan. His army was fatigued and worn down by their long, difficult, and rapid marches;

and the thought of retracing their steps over the same ground, every part of the route marked by disappointment and disaster, with little hope of better fortune, was discouraging in the extreme. Yet his officers differed in opinion. Some thought, and very sensibly too, that they had better go back to South Carolina and keep what they had gained by two years of hard fighting, than to try their fortune on new fields, and further urging that if they did not go to the assistance of their garrisons in South Carolina these would inevitably be over-come ; just as you have seen that they were. But Cornwallis decided for a Virginia campaign, hoping, with Clinton's co-operation from New York, that he would find better fortune for the British arms. After a most tedious and diffi-cult march of three hundred miles through North Carolina he reached Petersburgh, where he took command of all the British forces in Virginia.

"Virginia had been for some time desolated by a band of British marauders under Benedict Arnold, who wreaked his vengeance on its de-fenseless inhabitants without measure or mercy. Washington had sent La Fayette there to hold the monster in check, and cover the homes and heads of the terrified women and children. On

one occasion they had nearly succeeded in capturing him, but he escaped. He afterward inquired of an American officer who was in his
camp under a flag of truce, 'What would you
have done with me if you had caught me?'
He answered promptly, 'We should have buried
with every mark of honor that one of your legs
which was wounded in our service ; the rest of
your body we should have hanged.'

" Seeing that Virginia was now to become the
scene of warfare between the contending armies,
Washington laid his plans accordingly. He
called a council of American and French land
and naval officers. Intelligence was received
just at this time that the Count de Grasse
would soon arrive with reinforcements of land
and sea forces. Two plans were discussed :
the capture of New York, and the siege of
Yorktown, where Cornwallis had intrenched
himself. These plans were fully debated. To
take New York was by far the most difficult
and tedious work, and the Count de Grasse, by
instructions of the French government, could
remain only a limited time in American waters.
The capture of Cornwallis and his army appeared entirely possible within that time, and
the Virginia campaign was decided upon. They
gave out, however, that they intended to attack

New York; for Washington wished to mislead Clinton, so that he might keep his forces for its defense, instead of sending reinforcements to Cornwallis. Washington wrote letters concerning his plans of attack, and purposely let them fall into British hands. All the dispositions of his troops were made to favor this design; he even caused a large army bakery to be erected on the New Jersey coast. Clinton was completely deceived. The French fleets put out to sea as if to maneuver, and Washington led his army into New Jersey, and marched as far as Trenton on the Delaware. Here he paused, giving out that he wished to draw Clinton out of his intrenchments. Clinton was very wise, and kept his doors fast locked.

"Washington knew that as soon as he passed the Delaware all disguises must be dropped, as Clinton could no longer doubt his real intentions. He waited until he received intelligence that the French fleet had reached the coasts of Virginia. He then instantly put his army in motion; they crossed the Delaware, and ran rather than marched through Pennsylvania to the head of the Chesapeake Bay. Not finding adequate transports they marched to Annapolis, where the French fleet received them and landed them near Williamsburgh. Finding the

French fleet had disappeared from Newport, the British Admiral Graves immediately put to sea and steered for the Chesapeake. He had heard nothing, of course, of the expected French fleet under De Grasse, and only thought to encounter the fleet under De Barras. Finding them both, however, and knowing how fatal it would be to allow the French to remain masters of the Chesapeake, he bravely prepared for battle. The battle went sorely against him, and he was obliged to convey his shattered vessels back to New York for repairs.

"You may imagine Clinton's vexation upon finding how completely he had been outwitted. In order to attract Washington's attention, and, if possible, draw off his forces from Virginia, he planned an expedition of fire, plunder, and murder into Connecticut, putting Arnold in command. The destruction and suffering were without parallel, but Washington would not stir a man from before Yorktown.

"The Americans had drawn around Cornwallis a circle of batteries, which was soon to be a circle of fire. He hoped to be able, however, to hold out until Clinton could detach an army and fleet to his succor. He received a letter in cipher stating that the fleet would sail from New York not later than October 5, and urging him to hold out. So the British worked industriously to strengthen their defenses ; the Americans and French worked quite as briskly, advancing their parallels, and erecting batteries, which they crowned with more than one hundred heavy guns. The 5th of October came, but no signs of the fleet. The fire of the French and American gunners had been given with fatal precision and effect, and many of the British defenses were battered into rubbish. Day after day passed. The repairs of the British fleet at New York were still uncompleted, notwithstanding Clinton's extreme anxiety for the safety of Cornwallis. Another letter came saying they would surely sail on the 12th of October. Cornwallis began to despair. He beheld battery after battery dismantled, their walls of defense crumbling under the well-directed fire of the allies. Two strong redoubts remained to be taken. Washington ordered an assault, assigning one to the French and the other to the Americans. The Americans were led by the Marquis de La Fayette and Colonel Alexander Hamilton, one of Washington's aides, and a young man of brilliant promise, who in after life fulfilled all the promise of his youth. The French were led by able and enthusiastic young French officers. There was great emulation

between the French and American soldiers as
to which should first gain possession of the
redoubt assigned to them. Their officers addressed them a few words of inspiration ; the
attack was made with the greatest impetuosity, and the redoubts carried at the point
of the bayonet, with little loss of life on either
side.

" This achievement brought great glory both
to French and Americans, and Washington presented the French regiments with the cannon
which crowned the redoubt they had carried.
Cornwallis, seeing only ruin before him, and
beholding the sufferings of his men, now
crowded into a small space, more than two
thousand disabled by wounds and camp fever,
which raged among them, listened to the advice
of his officers, and resolved to attempt an escape. On the night of the 18th of October the
plan was attempted. The sick and wounded
were left with a letter to Washington from Cornwallis, recommending them to his mercy and
generosity, notwithstanding the monstrous cruelties the British were at this very moment
perpetrating in Connecticut. The largest part
of the British army safely embarked in small
boats to cross the James river, when a most unexpected and violent squall arose, driving the

boats down the river, and threatening them with instant destruction.

"With great difficulty they succeeded in re-landing, and returned to their camp feeling that the decrees of Providence were against them. On the morning of October 19, 1781, Cornwallis, perceiving their condition past all remedy, sent a flag to Washington, and proposals to appoint commissioners to arrange for capitulation. ' The posts of York and Gloucester were surrendered on the 19th of October. The land forces became prisoners to America and the seamen to France. The officers retained their arms and baggage. All the shipping and naval stores fell to the French. The Americans took the field artillery—one hundred and sixty pieces of cannon. The prisoners amounted to over seven thousand. The talents and bravery displayed in this siege by the allies won them immortal glory, and they enhanced it by the humanity and generosity with which they treated their prisoners. The French officers in particular honored themselves by the most delicate behavior. Lord Cornwallis, in his public letters, acknowledged in warm terms the magnanimity of this conduct.'

"The fleet that Clinton was to send to their relief left New York on the 19th of October,

the very day of the capitulation. Arriving at
the mouth of the Chesapeake they learned the
real state of affairs, sorrowfully turned their
ships' prows, and carried the evil tidings back to
New York. You can readily imagine the national rejoicings over so great a victory. There
was no longer any doubt concerning the triumph
of the republican cause. This great disaster,
following upon the expulsion of the British army
from the Southern States, would certainly de-
termine the British Ministry to cease the struggle of arms.

"The names of Washington, Rochambeau, De
Grasse, and La Fayette were on every tongue.
Congress addressed thanks alike to generals,
officers, and soldiers, distributing to Washington and the French officers the standards
and cannon captured during the siege. 'The
Congress repaired in a body to one of the
churches in Philadelphia to render their thanks
to the most high God for this victory, and also
appointed the 13th of December as a day of
prayer and acknowledgment for so signal an
evidence of Divine protection.' The State legislatures, the universities, and the literary socie-
ties also addressed Washington, 'The sincere
homage of their felicitations and admiration, to
which he answered with exemplary modesty

that he had done no more than what his duty required of him. He was eloquent in extolling the valor of the army, and the assistance of an ally no less generous than powerful!'

" When the news arrived in England a general sentiment of hopeless consternation filled the land. They were heartily weary of a war which had been unpopular from the first with the English people, and which had piled up the national debt and burdened the people until their patience was exhausted. They clamored for a change of Ministers who could treat with America for peace. So great was the pressure that Lord North at last resigned, making way for more peaceful counsels.

" No other military events occurred in America, but the war still raged between England and France, Spain, and Holland, on the high seas for a year longer ; but having attained the chief object of going to war, namely, the separation of the American colonies from England, France also inclined to peace.

" In the year 1782, at Paris, the several treaties were signed between England and America, and between England and the European powers. The most important conditions of the treaty between England and America was that the king of England acknowledge the liberty, sovereignty, and independence of the · thirteen United States of America, which were all named successively. Imaginary lines of boundary were agreed upon which brought within the territory of the United States immense countries, lakes, and rivers, to which up to that time they had never pretended any sort of claim.

" Thus gloriously ended the long and desperate struggle of our American Fathers for their national liberties. And now, children, I will conclude this story with one of the grandest scenes the history of the world affords. I have told you again and again how the fame of Washington had spread into all lands, because of his devotion to his country—a devotion which had been subjected to the severest test and had been found pure. But the days of peril and struggle were ended, and now the world held its breath as it looked on to see whether Washington would selfishly wear his laurels for his own glory, or whether these, too, were to be laid on the altar of his country. In the hour of triumph and power, the idol of the army and of the nation, no dream of personal aggrandizement ruffled the calm of his noble soul. The Christian hero had done his work in the spirit of that divine Master who came not to be ministered unto but to minister. He had already received a reward from that Master, and bore it with him in his own bosom, unseen by mortal eye. No marvel, then, that earthly honors seemed to him as the dust in the balance ; they could not lure him from the path of duty. He had a longing for the sweet rest of his own fireside, but no hunger for the honor that cometh of men.

" Peace had been declared, and its fruits secured to his country, but the supreme power conferred upon him by Congress still remained in the hands of Washington. He therefore communicated to that body, then in session in the city of Annapolis, in Maryland, his resolution to resign his command, and requested to know if it would be their pleasure to receive his resignation in writing, or at an audience. The Congress replied, and appointed the 23d of December for that ceremony. On that day the hall was crowded with the noble spirits of the young republic. The legislative and executive officials of Congress and of the various States, officers of the army, distinguished foreign officers, and the consul-general of France, were present. At the hour designated the general was introduced by the secretary, and conducted to a seat near the President. A profound silence reigned ; the members of

Congress remained seated, and the spectators stood with uncovered heads. After an interval, the President, General Mifflin, informed him that the United States, in Congress assembled, were ready to receive his communications.

" Washington rose, and with inexpressible dignity delivered the following address :—

" ' MR. PRESIDENT :—The great events on which my resignation depended having at length taken place, I have now the honor of offering my sincere congratulations to Congress, and presenting myself before them to surrender into their hands the trust committed to me, and to claim the indulgence of retiring from the service of my country.

" ' Happy in the confirmation of our independence and sovereignty, and pleased with the opportunity afforded the United States of becoming a respectable nation, I resign with satisfaction the appointment I accepted with diffidence ; a diffidence in my abilities to accomplish so arduous a task, which, however, was superseded by a confidence in the rectitude of our cause, the support of the supreme power of the Union, and the patronage of Heaven.

" ' The successful termination of the war has verified the most sanguine expectations ;

and my gratitude for the interposition of Providence and the assistance I have received from my countrymen increases with every review of the momentous contest.

"'While I repeat my obligation to the army in general, I should do injustice to my own feelings not to acknowledge, in this place, the peculiar services and distinguished merits of the gentlemen who have been attached to my person during the war. It was impossible that the choice of confidential officers to compose my family should have been more fortunate. Permit me, sir, to recommend in particular those who have continued in service to the present moment as worthy of the favorable notice and patronage of Congress.

"'I consider it an indispensable duty to close this last solemn act of my official life by commending the interests of our dearest country to the protection of Almighty God, and those who have the superintendence of them to his holy keeping.

"'Having now finished the work assigned me, I retire from the great theater of action; and, bidding an affectionate farewell to this august body, under whose orders I have so long acted, I here offer my commission and take my leave of all the employments of public life.'"

" Having thus spoken, Washington advanced to the president, and deposited his commission in his hands.

" The president, on behalf of the Congress, made the following reply :—

"' Sir : The United States, in Congress assembled, receive with emotions too affecting for utterance the solemn resignation of the authorities under which you have led their troops with success through a perilous and a doubtful war. Called upon by your country to defend its invaded rights, you accepted the sacred charge before it had formed alliances, and while it was without funds or a government to support you. You have conducted the great military contest with wisdom and fortitude, invariably regarding the rights of the civil power through all disasters and changes. You have, by the love and confidence of your fellow-citizens, enabled them to display their martial genius and transmit their fame to posterity. You have persevered till these United States, aided by a magnanimous king and nation, have been enabled, under a just Providence, to close the war in freedom, safety, and ·independence, on which happy event we sincerely join you in congratulations.

21

" ' Having defended the standard of liberty in this new world, having taught a lesson useful to those who inflict and to those who feel oppression, you retire from the great theater of action with the blessings of your fellow-citizens ; but the glory of your virtues will not terminate with your military command : it will continue to animate remotest ages.

" ' We feel with you our obligations to the army in general, and will particularly charge ourselves with the interests of those confidential officers who have attended your person to this affecting moment.

" ' We join you in commending the interest of our dearest country to the protection of Almighty God, beseeching him to dispose the hearts and minds of its citizens to improve the opportunity afforded them of becoming a happy and respectable nation. And for you we address to him our earnest prayers that a life so beloved may be fostered with all his care, that your days may he happy as they have been illustrious, and that he will finally give you that reward which this world cannot give.'

"At the conclusion of this address a long and profound silence pervaded the Chamber. Each soul was filled with the greatness of the hour; for in the exaltation of this man all the race were lifted up. Immediately after, Washington sought the long-desired repose of his beautiful home on the banks of the Potomac."

THE END.

www.ingramcontent.com/pod-product-compliance
Lightning Source LLC
Chambersburg PA
CBHW020808060726
47498CB00017B/1015